Lost: Midnight Mist

By

Steven M. Mellerson

A Dante's Paradise Book

Published by Dante's Paradise Publishing

1983 Crotona Ave. 2nd Fl.

Bronx, NY 10457, USA

First Printing, August 2008

Mellerson, Steven M.

Lost: Midnight Mist / Steven M. Mellerson. – 1st ed.

ISBN 978-0-615-24978-0

Prologue

Unabashed the Devil stood making his mock of me;
While round him barked the mad and hungry dogs as
he laughed in his gaiety; I wept as a child would
for naught, save The Beast, was there for me to
see; My will is shred and forsaken, I am undone
by eternal blasphemy; In his wake I lay strewn,
my soul rent asunder, condemned, I still weep for
he has defeated me.

    I died. There was no life flashing before
my eyes. There were no harps. There were no
white robes. There was no land of milk and
honey. There were no wings…
…Well, maybe I was wrong about the wings, but
there was definitely no peace, not for a while
anyway. Sound confusing? I know, I still don't
quite understand it myself, but it was an
incredible adventure.

Where should I start? Perhaps at the beginning...
I always wanted to be an archaeologist... No! That
would take forever. Let's start more recently.
Ah, yes, the Guardian.

   As you may have already guessed I became an
archaeologist, just like my father, Nicco Troy.
I must have gotten my sense of adventure from
him, because like him, I more often than not,
chose thrill over self-preservation, and I only
surrounded myself with people just as insane as I
am... was.

   I went from the deepest, darkest jungles of
Africa to the highest most frigid caves of the
Himalayas. My exploits were becoming legend. I
was the standard to which the younger generations
aspired to, and the one that the older ones
hated. The signs were all around me. You
always hear people talk about never knowing when
your time is up. But you know. Somewhere deep
inside, where our ancestors knew instinctively
that if you stray from the group, what is out in
the dark will get you. It's beyond thought and
more basic than any emotion.

   I knew but I ignored all the signs around
me. I wanted so much to be like my father. And
now I'm just like him.

   Dead...

CHAPTER ONE

Someone was banging on my door. In all
honesty they were probably gently rapping at it,
but due to the 7am-ness of the situation I
elevated it to rudely hammering at my door. I
was, at that point, half way through dreaming and
waking up and I couldn't tell what was real yet.
I opened my eyes just enough to see that the
covers were half way down my body and my naked
breasts were exposed to the cool morning air.
His arm was lying across my stomach, solid and
muscular, but as I found out last night
surprisingly soft. He snuggled his face against
me, and he was warm, almost feverish, but it felt
so good that I wanted to just wrap him around me
and live there.

The knocking continued, more insistent, and
that, at last, yanked me out of the afterglow I
was thoroughly enjoying. I realized what had

happened last night with a start. Did I actually do that? Did I agree to this? David groaned and that answered that question. It did happen otherwise there wouldn't be this man, naked, cuddled up against me. I needed to get away at least for a second, just to think. Finally, I registered the pounding (read: politely, knocking) at the door, damn they were persistent.

I pulled him up to me and kissed him, a soft brush of lips, "David, could you get that please?"

He got up and as he stood there, naked with the sun shining in on him, the light played across his chest and abs to great advantage, just looking at that wonderful body again made things low in my own body tight. Well that explains some of it. He wrapped the sheet around himself.

"Sita, last night, you said that you would marry me." He said face blank, gauging my reaction to it being said out loud.

I had to kiss him to reassure him that I was okay with it, even if deep inside it might be a lie. I didn't want to make the classic girl mistake of assuming that a man's feelings can't be hurt just as easily as a woman's. If I care about his feelings this much I must have made the right decision. Right?

"Yea I did," I said. The look in his eyes was so intimate heat rushed up my face and I realized that I was blushing, something only he can make me do.

"Do you regret it?" He asked and his face still empty, giving nothing away.

That was it, that was what I needed to think about, and I realized that he wasn't going to let me. I looked up in to those chocolate brown eyes and wanted to lie but I couldn't, "No, I don't regret it."

I realized, just then, that it was true; I didn't regret it and that made me smile. He rewarded my correct answer with that brilliant smile that melted me to my toes. The knocking turned into full out banging and he finally made and about face to see who it was. When he came back into the room he was holding an envelope.

He tossed me the letter; it had "CERTIFIED" stamped across it in big block letters. I read the name of the sender, Joshua Troy. My stomach tightened at that name. I tore open the letter and read:

Hey Sita,

Been a while hasn't it? I hear you're doing big things Mr. Jones or would that be Lara Croft. You know I get those pop culture

*references all mixed up. Just so you don't
crumple this up and throw it away let me get to
the point. I found something very interesting
that might take your expertise to confirm, but if
it is what I think then it'd be like finding Big
Foot using the Holy Grail as a pimp cup. You know
where to meet me.*

Josh

If I had any common sense I would have
thrown it away and continued to go about my very,
very good life. But my explorer's curiosity got
the better of me and I knew I had to go meet this
man.

The letter had soured my mood just a little
because the last time I heard from Joshua I found
out my mother was dead. Which I guess would sour
anyone's mood. David saw the look on my face and
even knew why I was wearing it. So he made a
very generous offer, at least he thought so.
"Hey why don't we take a shower and go meet
Joshua."

I had to smile at that, "We? One night of
okay sex and you think you can just hop in the
shower with me?"

He pouted, but it was false because it
didn't reach his eyes. No, his eyes held a very

different look, more salacious, like he knew exactly what he did to me and I couldn't undermine it even if I tried. What he said was, "Just okay?"

My smile turned into a complete dopey I'm-so-in-love-with-you-I-can't-contain-myself grin.

"We can't," I said sheepishly.

"Oh I think we can, over and over again. We proved that last night."

I giggled, an honest to God giggle. I never giggle. I had to leave the room before I made more of an ass out of myself for love.

God I love him...

Stop it.

He pouted again, but I still managed, begrudgingly I might add, to turn down the tandem shower otherwise I would never get out the house. That excuse brought that damned smile back and I groaned and had to leave or I just might have agreed to marry him again.

After I was fresh and clean I slipped into some light blue jeans, a white polo shirt, and some white Nikes. After all anything but white was not appropriate for the hell on earth also known as summers in New York.

The letter had stated very plainly that he needed a team to go after his treasure and no one

else wanted to go on a suicide mission so I was
it. Thing about suicide missions is as long as
you don't mind dying you were going to be richer
than God. Oh, and to meet him at Smokey's Diner.
Only the two of us still called it Smokey's. It
was a restaurant that I knew well. I came here
everyday as a kid. The owner, Smokey, knew me by
name and it wasn't an act of God for me to get a
free meal or two when I was a broke college
student. But I haven't been here since Smokey
died and his kid's sold it to a soulless coffee
giant frequented by the yuppie Manhattanites.

I walk through the front door and memories
came flooding back. The booths still ran along
the window but the old burgundy leather was
changed into that artificial plastic stuff that
is never as comfortable. The smell of
Hamburgers, onions, and beer was changed into
Mocha Lattes and briefcase leather. They kept
the set up but the spirit of Smokey's was gone.
I knew implicitly where he'd be sitting, the same
place we always sat. We saw each other at the
same time.

He reclined his long body like a big cat and
gave me that slow lazy smile of his before
saying, "Hiya' sis, it's been a while hasn't it."

"Ten years, Joshua. It's been ten years."

"Haven't seen you since… What, mom's funeral?" that made me wince, "How have you been?"

As much as I resisted it I missed my little brother. It's been ten years because I can see my father's face looking back at me whenever I look at him. Guilt is a multi-splendored thing, isn't it? Yea I was a bad sister.

We spent some time catching up; I told him that I'm engaged and that I am a famed and envied archeologist, how arrogant I know but it doesn't make it less true. From his letter, however, I don't think I needed to mention the latter. He told me how he was doing big things. He'd made tons of money selling ancient artifacts and relics to museums and private collectors around the world. It was good catching up for a minute but then that discomfort that usually set in when I spent too much time with my brother… well, set in. When uncomfortable, focus on business. That's my motto.

"So, why did you send me this letter?"

CHAPTER TWO

Joshua pulled out a portion of a map, brown and decaying, of an area I knew all too well. Etched in one corner of the map was a shining crimson jewel.

"Where did you find this?" I asked trying not to drool.

"Well, you know how you made me keep all of dad's things?" He asked.

"You found this in there?"

"No. I had never been up to it, but my maid had been cleaning and she decided to organize for me… " His voice trailed off.

I held the map in my hands. The texture was familiar but not paper or parchment. It had a dry waxy feel too it. I knew what the parchment was made from, and the brown etching confirmed it. The map was made of dried animal flesh. I refused to speculate as to what kind. And I am fairly certain that the brown "ink" wasn't ink at all. It was a map of a path through a jungle to a temple. I knew this jungle, also. I'd been there only once before, and something had always kept me from going back. We had been there one time with our father. It had been the last time either of us saw him. Maybe that was it.

"You want to go after the Heart?"

"Yes. I want to go after the Heart."

The Heart of Khan was a magnificent ruby that Genghis Khan wore on his cloak. It's what made him such a fierce ruler and supposedly rendered him unkillable. When he died of unknown causes in the early 13th century it had been lost, and it wasn't until my father found this map that there was talk that it might be in the jungles of the Philippine Islands. It is said that the heart is protected by an indestructible juggernaut, simply named The Guardian. The mythology didn't interest me, only the thrill of adventure, the exhilaration of danger, and the call of my father's life's work. It was the treasure that my father died trying to find.

As much as I would like to blame him or anyone else for the outcome of this particular venture it was I who spent weeks assembling the team, and researching the locale. I was fully enthused and no amount of foreboding was going to change my mind.

The day of our flight everyone assembled on the runway for a last inspection. I personally assembled a team of the most insane thrill seekers on the planet, each one an innovator and master of his or her craft as well as close friends. We were a surrogate family of misfits among our peers. No one liked us and that's how we liked it. Besides they were just jealous.

Jillian Thomas, the only other woman on this trip was my engineer and pilot. She has a double Masters in Engineering and Computer Engineering and can pretty much MacGyver her way out of any situation.

There was Daniel Harvey, ex-Navy SEAL, bodyguard and all around badass. He's almost a foot taller than me which puts him well over six feet. I would never arm wrestle him but I would always trust him at my back. His loyalty was absolute and it never hurts to have some muscle who knows a little something about explosives.

My brother, a human world's languages dictionary, was along. I know seven different languages but he makes me look like an idiot child with how easily he picks up other dialects. Finally David and I rounded out the group.

I usually ignore that cold sinking feeling in the pit of my stomach I get before every mission because that is a good way to not get famous. With the work we do you should be afraid. It means that when you succeed you are all the more famous. But the butterflies in my stomach this time were vicious and rabid. So I slept to ignore it.

I rarely dream on these flights but I do now and I wish I hadn't.

The rain falls in sheets. I'm crying in great heaping sobs as a man scoops me up off of the ground. Mud and leaves clinging stubbornly to my new dress. I remember that making it so much worse. The dress was a gift from daddy. I ground my face into his shoulder so that my brother doesn't see me lose it. How undignified, ugh.

"Sita… Sita? Where's daddy? You were with him weren't you? Why didn't he come back with you?" he asks.

In a voice thick with tears I reply, "Don't worry Joshua I will protect you from now on. It's you and me forever ok Josh?"

"Ok, Sita. I love you big sister," he said with a smile.

"I love you too, little brother."

I woke up on the plane as we were landing; dried streams ran down my face. I looked over and Joshua is there excited like a child on Christmas morning.

David tapped me, "We're here Sita," and in a lower voice he told me, "you were whimpering in your sleep. Are you up to this?"

"Yea of course I am," I said voice thick, not with tears, but sleep. Really, just sleep.

"Good cause there ain't no going back now. Get ready."

I stepped off of the plane and this airport was just like any other, modern and state of the art, but apparently the only difference was that this one was on the surface of the sun. The sweat beaded on my forehead and I could feel it trail down my back. I had forgotten how hot it was in Manila this time of year.

After procuring a couple of guides and some hands to help with the dig we took a speed boat to Batangas, which is a few hours away from Manila and composed of dense forest, wholly uncharted.

Batangas has a couple of villages on the outskirts of the jungle. The locals don't dare risk wandering too far into these jungles. Each person we passed knew who we were and what we were planning on doing. They have seen it all before. With all there local folklore and legends the superstitions were deep rooted and real. For them these forests were cursed. Luckily enough for me I had courage powered by good old American skepticism, so off to see the wizard.

CHAPTER THREE

Most people have no idea what a jungle is. I mean, they have this abstract image in their head that it's hot and thick with trees and animals, but that doesn't even come close to describing what a jungle is at all. A jungle is a force of nature all on its own, alive. It is alive the way that any predator is alive. It breathes. It sees. It hunts and kills. If you don't respect the jungle you don't make it out.

The heat was pressing against the back of my neck as we marched through the trees. David took point, clearing a path, not so much cutting one with a machete as giving himself over to the trees cutting only when necessary. He was always so at home in the jungle. It was as if the trees moved out of his way.

This trek would have been like any other trek through the jungle except something was off.

The closer we got to the temple the more I felt we shouldn't be here. I looked at the others so see if it was just me. It wasn't. The locals that we got to help us were huddle together speaking in a language I didn't know. They were speaking quickly almost frantic.

"Something about this place doesn't feel right," I said to David.

"I know what you mean," he replied, "Do you hear that?"

I listened.

"No."

"Exactly. I don't hear anything but us. We're in the middle of the jungle and I don't hear any birds, wind, streams, there are no sounds of any kind. The jungle is quiet as the grave. It's never this quiet in the jungle."

My brother, Joshua came over to me and said, "I don't feel right about this mission. The villagers over there are protesting going any further. They say this ground is tainted with death. Old death like what ever is here has been killing for a very long time and its desire for it is soaked into the very ground."

The only excuse I have for what I said next is that I was scared and that what he said is exactly how I was feeling. "What's wrong with you," I replied, "how many missions do you think I've been on. Do you think we get famous by turning back because a few locals have some scary fables?"

"No, but…"

"Then what makes you think I'm gonna turn back now."

"But Sita maybe there is something to that Guardian thing. I think…"

"I'm not paying you to think. I'm paying you to translate."

"But…"

"So translate this to them. They weren't complaining when they were taking our money, so they and you can shut the fuck up and stop being such pussies. This could be the greatest event in our careers. We're making history, and I'm not jeopardizing that for your gutlessness. They and you need to grow a pair and stop being such bitches."

I told you I was a bad sister.

The moment I said it I wish I hadn't. The look in his eyes was so full of hurt that I would have given anything at that moment to chase it away. But I didn't.

We walked the rest of the way in complete silence, I told myself that I was going to apologize for what I said when were safely back on the plane. That was all I thought about until the jungle broke and we emerged into a grove and at its center loomed an ancient temple, with striking familiarity. A chill shot through my body and a feeling of nostalgia came over me as if I had been here before.

David saw me and asked, "You okay, love?" But something tells me that he had been talking for awhile but I hadn't heard a word of what he said.

"Yea I'm fine, just a bit of déjà vu."

The temple was covered with overgrown brush; it looked like nobody had been here for decades. We made our way to the back of the temple where all that stood in our way were two enormous stone doors. This made me nervous because there were no obstacles or traps, no carvings and no second exit. There was nothing but the two stone doors. It was as if the architect were building a prison instead of a temple. Maybe that is just my fear projecting. Inscribed on the doors in Baybayin, an ancient form of Tagalog, a simple warning:

"*To Those That Desire Riches and Grace, Beware The Guardian Awaits.*"

When I opened the doors a red glimmer shone from the back of the chamber. The glow sparkled off of all the jewels and gold; the majesty was far beyond any of our wildest fantasies.

The ground was littered with the treasure of centuries untold and the bodies of failed attempts, but while my men were preoccupied by the sights around them I was drawn to the back of the temple, to the eerie crimson glow. The shine was haunting because even though it illuminated the room with no apparent source of energy there was only darkness that surrounded it. The shadows were thick like the densest fog. When I touched the glowing stone the darkness peeled back like a cape being flung aside.

When I came in contact it flashed bright as a captive star made of garnet, and when it did it lit all the dormant torches that hung from the walls. The light made us quickly aware of what awaited us behind that darkness. All there really was for us to claim from that chamber was our destiny. Death was there to be paid his due.

Resting on a solid gold throne was an immense sentinel, clad in scarlet and ebony armor and wrapped in chains. The chains were connect end to end with two colossal blades that rested across the beast's shoulders, as amazing and terrifying as this situation had become all I was focused on was what lay embedded in the titan's chest.

He stood up; towering over us all and said only one thing, "I am Guardian and your end is come. Time to DIE!"

With a lightning quick gesture he whipped the chain and it coiled itself around Joshua and lifted him into the air. That snapped me out of my daze and I screamed, "NO!"

He moved with a grace something of his size had no business of possessing. It was like a great cat and a dancer combined. It was almost like he was swimming through the air. It was unnerving.

I tried to help him but David stopped me. "No! Let go of me David!"

"You'll be killed," he warned.

"Sita…?" Joshua called to me.

"No! Stop it, please… I'm supposed to protect him! He's my little brother…"

The blade seemed to awaken like a mighty snake beckoned by its master. My eyes were instantly hot and my chest tight with the urge to scream. It all happened in slow motion. The blade glided toward Joshua's head like it was barely moving at all. But that wasn't right. I think my sense of time had dilated from shock.

Once the Guardian decapitated my brother then crushed his body like an over ripened fruit time went back to normal.

No… actually it seemed to speed up as if it needed to work a little harder to get back to normal. He tossed Joshua away like some useless refuse.

"He's all I have…" squeezed out of me in a choked whisper.

I dropped to my knees, my whole body trembling and did nothing. Even when my exterior seems calm, I have never stopped crying over my brother. All my men opened fire and he shrugged the bullets off like gnats and worked his way through us like a butcher sent by Satan himself.

The gun blasts in the small chamber were like deafening concussion grenades and it made the screams seem miles away. Their bodies smacked the ground with wet plops and it laughed. The blood rained down over the chamber like a gruesome spring shower.

All who were left was David and me. Dread, the feeling of imminent doom, filled me. I knew that it was time for me to die. The Guardian had had its fun and now he wanted to end it, he began to twirl the chain. He spun it faster and faster until all you could see was a golden blur.

David pulled from his side his machete and made some distance between him and me. The Guardian threw the blade at David with so much power it was like it was shot from a cannon. David rolled to the side and the shining weapon struck the ground with devastating force.

The blade chased David around the room always inches from killing my love. But David had always been supernaturally swift. He made a sharp turn and ran straight at the Guardian with a battle cry, the machete poised to strike. The blade came, spinning back, toward David.

I shut my eyes and screamed, "NO!!!"

Then everything was silence. When I opened my eyes the Guardian was lying on its side with the blade plunged hilt deep into the Heart. It was leaking some sparkling red fluid on the ground. David was on one knee.

I ran to my fiancé and put my hand on his shoulder and he coughed up blood and fell to all fours. He looked at me with bloody tears welling in his eyes. He held on to himself, his whole body was oddly still, as if he were afraid of what would happen if he moved.

He spoke around blood thick in his throat, his last words, "Sita I love yo… Oh my God! Run,

run for your life, please, plea…" then burst into an ungainly tangle of arms and legs.

His blood was all I could see as it splashed on my face and crept around my knees, warm, almost hot with the adrenaline.

The heat behind my eyes that had already been there exploded into hot streams down my face. When I turned around looming over me in all his diabolical grandeur was The Guardian. I tried to scream but he gripped his massive hand over my face and lifted me high into the air. He brought my face close to his. I looked into his eyes and they were just black wells. I felt myself fall down, impossibly down, into those black pits.

I was cold and lonely and the only warmth was the tears running hot and steady down my face. His grip on my face tightened and I suddenly couldn't breathe, but before I had the chance to suffocate he snapped my neck with a flick of his wrist, and so I died.

CHAPTER FOUR

There was darkness, followed by a blinding light. Next my eyes opened, and every thing was clearer than it had ever been. So clear, that I could distinguish the spaces between the cracks in the stone walls on the far side of the chamber. Everything had changed, yet stayed the same. Statues seemed to move, but didn't. It's something that no human can ever know.

The Guardian stood among what was left of our bodies, reveling in his victory. He'd removed the blade from his Heart and it was as unmarred as when we'd first arrived. His bellow clipped short and he looked down. An arm was sticking out of his chest. He followed the arm up to the body to the eyes and there was this look on his face as he stared at me. It was a look of confusion like he couldn't understand what was happening to him. I didn't understand

the look. Everyone dies, why was he so
surprised it was happening to him?

I tore the heart from his body, and watched
as his body convulsed like he was having a grand
mal seizure or dying from strychnine poisoning.
He decayed right before my very eyes. His body
shrunk in on itself as if he were dying of
consumption. The near skeletal remains exploded
into black and scarlet motes and he was gone from
this world as if he'd never existed.

I licked the blood from my fingers, and then
the realization of what just happened flooded
into me. I took a deep shaking breath in
preparation then dropped to my knees to let out
one long ragged scream after another.

I looked at the blood on my hands.

I shrieked as if I could scream the pain out
of me.

I looked at the carnage all around me.

I screamed long, hopeless, pitiful screams.

I looked to my fiancé who was nothing more
than so much ground meat.

And nothing more came out but hoarse
squeaks.

Finally, I threw up and the world went all
Starry Night. Blackness ate at the edges of my
vision then there was nothingness again.

When I regained consciousness there were dried streams that ran down the sides of my face. As I was recovering from the grogginess of unconsciousness I got up and stumbled outside to the jungle. The sun was low in the sky stuck between twilight and true dark.

I began to feel something rise to the surface, swimming up through me frantically like a diver deep under the surface desperate for air. I closed my eyes and I could almost see it as a pit. An expanse so dark it was like an inky ocean of blackness. It was filled with shimmering color like an oil slick.

I thought, *"How could something be so dark and shimmer,"* but the thought faded as something rose up out of the darkness.

It was nothing I could see with my eyes, but that didn't make it any less real. It began to pace in the darkness like some giant predator pacing its cage at the zoo. You could sense it was something that wasn't used to being trapped. It knew freedom and it would be damned if it stayed captive. Like any animal not yet broken it tested its boundaries, it slashed the bars of its cage. The problem is that that cage was me.

The pain didn't build it exploded. I was suddenly overcome with agony so immense by spine bowed while I was still standing. I didn't so much collapse as my body slammed into the ground as if I had fallen from a great height. It wasn't a sharp pain or burning or any kind of pain that I had words for. It just was. It existed as the pure essence of anguish. I offered my body the only release I could think of.

I screamed.

It was a piercing shriek of a sound that my human throat had never been able to make. It was a sound like something that would come out of a leopard but that wasn't exactly it either, and I could swear that under that there were the distant screams of thousands other of people; it swept over the land like a great tempest and it sent birds fluttering.

My own voice brought something to my attention the absence of sound that I remember from walking through this jungle was no more. It was like everything was in hyper-focus. I could hear the fluttering heart beat of the birds flying away. I could hear the quickening breath of the small animals in the trees as if they could sense a predator near.

Sight had become secondary; the night was alive with sounds and smells. I could smell the

animals creeping just behind the trees like some
curtain covering a buffet. I could have
everything out here. Own it in a way that human
beings rarely think about owning things anymore.

My outburst must have attracted some
attention because I could hear one more thing the
rhythmic march of visitors. But as loud as the
breathing and stomping was it was distant
somewhere behind that curtain of arboreal
infinity. I said out loud in barely a whisper
how I could own all that beautiful life because,
own, was too complicated a concept. But there
was something else something much simpler that
they could be.

"Prey…"

I gave myself over to the jungle like you do
to water when you are swimming. And the same as
water the trees flowed around me in that liquid
grace. I was suddenly aware of every stone and
stump, every root and branch. I flowed through
the trees like a ghost or the wind or something
equally as intangible.

Once I began moving though I couldn't stop
or slow down or rather didn't want to. As a
matter of fact I just kept going faster and
faster. It felt so good to give myself over to
the movement. I was moving so fast that the

birds around me appeared to be suspended in mid-flight, and my speed was still increasing. I was unstoppable but just as I began to appreciate my new athletic achievement an obstacle.

"Humph... obstacle, ri-ight," I thought.

It was damn near a mountain.

Needless to say, I stopped but I stopped inches from the wall with out even a hint of slowing down. I wasn't breathing hard, winded, or tired in anyway. That was odd enough but it was what happened next that was the most disturbing.

I heard the footsteps and breathing again but this time they were accompanied by heartbeats many, many heartbeats. I heard them surround me, and salivating at the mouth. I could feel them; feel their need, their hunger. They were barely human just another kind of beast of the jungle.

I was surrounded by a horde of savages with blood on their breath, and I could guess what kind. They would like nothing better than to devour my flesh and keep my head as a trophy; however that was what we had in common. Disturbed yet?

I began to feel something, something that I had never felt before. It was not a good feeling; as a matter of fact, it was a very, very bad feeling. Heat rose up through my skin. It was like fire ants marching up and down my arms and across my back and face.

I could say I was filled with hatred, malice and contempt. But that didn't quite do it justice. The breeze felt cool against my hot skin because all that consumed me was pure rage.

My mind went to an empty place. It was that blackness in me, filled with nothing. No anger, no fear, no love, nothing just a kind of white noise, staticky. For a second I wondered if this was what it felt like to go crazy. If it was I could live with that.

I laughed. It was a deep throaty sound, touchable and close, full of promises meant for darkened bedrooms. It was a familiar sound that was never mine nor the words that followed, "Such a nice day for a bloodbath."

It was as if I stepped outside of myself and watched from afar as my body took control of itself in a merciless, bloody slaughter.

My eyes switched into slow motion, but that didn't mean that I did. Actually it was precisely the opposite. My movements were so quick that all they saw was a blur, a wave of invisible death. I became a death dealer and for them it came swift, cold, and brutal.

I repelled off of the rock with such force
that I was momentarily airborne. Traveling
though the air horizontally I gave the one
closest to me a blow to his chest with my feet.

I struck him with enough drive that I
crushed his breastbone, ribs, and the heart that
lie beneath. He flew back, hard, crushing the
three men that were behind him, finally slamming
into a tree and collapsing it onto the jungle
floor. I didn't waste the momentum, with
unnatural agility I twisted my body and mule
kicked the head off the man adjacent to him.

My body was instinctively moving in ways
that it had never moved. Upon landing I struck
three men in the throat crushing three
consecutive windpipes. My movements were as
fluid and elegant as a dance that I had practiced
thousands of times before. After that minor
display the smart ones ran, but they could not
escape my wrath. A battle ensued and they were
only the first victims.

I looked around sizing up my prey and it
looked as if they weren't moving at all. I had
enough time to carefully plan out how vicious to
be. And I planned to be incredibly vicious.

I took two heads and smashed them into a
third one; they dropped to the ground with their

brains hanging over their collars, moistening the grass with their blood. I relieved the fallen of their weapons: one hatchet, a ritual knife carved from human bone, and a razor sharp throwing disk.

I chucked the axe at the deserters and split them in half like firewood. Their blood splashed on the ground like warm water from a broken fire hose.

Next the razor disk, it had an interesting ricochet effect, cleaving multiple skulls like pudding before getting jammed in a tree. And then... there were three...

They bolted to the protection of the trees where they had the advantage.

"Yea...advantage."

I couldn't help but smirk at the prospect of them feeling safe among the trees. High above the ground I leapt through the canopy. I caught up to the first one with very little effort. I waited until he had stopped to rest then dropped straight down and sliced him in half with the bone-knife.

Back in the treetops I found the other one resting a few hundred yards away crying.

I could smell the fear on him like some bittersweet perfume. I knew that the fear made

the blood sweeter with adrenaline. I knew
exactly how it would taste. I don't know whose
memory I was channeling but I knew that I have
never thought of blood in that way. But the
sensory memory was so strong I had to blink twice
just to make sure I wasn't someplace else…
someone else.

I dropped down hanging from the branch with
my legs. He looked into my eyes and I was going
to let him live but suddenly flashes of him
murdering and gorging himself on innocent people
raced through my mind. The rage welled up inside
of me again and I snapped his head all the way
around and he slumped lifeless to the ground but
I had already caught up to the last one by that
time.

He was determined; he was still running. He
hadn't stopped once but he was not near fast
enough to evade me. I landed right on top of
him. He seemed to be headed for a clearing, a
village.

"Aw, too bad, you were almost there," I said
sarcastically, "You thought that you would be
safe among the trees, that if you could just get
back to your village you would escape me. Silly
rabbit…"

He started to whimper, "Ang Diyabla," he
continued to snivel; "I do not want to die."

My nails dug into the tender flesh of his
throat and a small stream of crimson fluid ran
down the side of my hand. I looked at the big
pulse in his throat. I watched it jump under the
surface like some trapped thing. I wanted to
help it free. The more I looked at his throat
the thinner his skin seemed to get. Until I
could smell the blood beneath the surface, hot
with fear. I felt a need so strong, a need that
didn't exactly have to do with sex or hunger but
something akin to both.

I looked at the blood I drew from him in a
new way, not as that vile necessity, but
something more inviting, more attractive. I
started to see food. Releasing my grip I tasted
the sweet nectar. It was incredible, I looked
down at him from atop his chest and bent forward
placing my lips inches from his quivering ear
lobe and grimly replied, "Then…you should have
never been born."

Once again the words aren't mine.

I sunk my teeth into his supple throat and
allowed the sweet flow to drain down into my
body. It was hot and thick. It tasted sweet and
metallic. I was entranced by it. I felt a pull

and the air became thick with something. It
pushed against me as I tried breath against it.
It was like a wall but there was nothing to see.
There was a pull to him and something inside me
pulled back. Then as that throb in his chest
slowed to a flutter I felt its grip grow weak and
with one last rasping exhale from him I pulled
all that power from both of us back into myself.
It was wondrous.

Suddenly, the tortuous assault returned.
It felt like something was trying to rip out of
me. This time, however, the pain manifested
itself in a more physical form. In one last
eruption of excruciating pain two enormous bat-
like wings burst from my back as if unfolding
from a thousand year sleep. Without warning I
shot up into the air and flew.

With a part of my brain that was beyond
thought I flew back home. By the time a thought
would form in my head that none of this should be
possible I landed in the courtyard of a Manhattan
apartment complex before I had the chance to
realize that I had even been flying.

I scanned the area and noticed a discarded
wall mirror. There I stood; I was 5'2, short
even for a woman. My hair was still straight
dark brown almost black. My skin, still that soft

tan, the color of coffee with lots of cream in it, I was still me but there was something decidedly unfamiliar. I would like to say it was the drying blood on my clothes and flecks of reddish brown spots on my face, but that wasn't it.

No it wasn't the fact that I looked fresh from the slaughter. It was the wings the same color as my skin, but larger than any wings I have ever seen. They looked like hairless bat wings; the large thin, yet muscular arms and long crooked fingers descending down the flesh connecting it all so paper-thin I could see the blue veins weaved through it.

That wasn't the only difference.

I had a tail waving, cordially, at me its movement was so fluid, not like any animal with a tail that I have ever seen, almost swimming through the air. It was thin but had a sense of power to it and topped with a point like an arrowhead. But the most disturbing of all the additions, yes even more than the wings, my toes were fused into hooves all shiny and black under the moon, finally topping it all off the most subtle of the changes the fangs in my mouth. I looked like a medieval painting.

I was a Devil. Yes, a capital D, Devil, at true manifestation of a demon. There I stood a beast, a monster. My ordeal in the jungle had left me changed.

What happened? I can't think… can't remember… I sat down and tried to think. But thinking wasn't a luxury I could afford at the moment. Just then, a menagerie of heartbeats approached me from behind, *"Damn!"* I had no idea what to do; all I could think was that I needed a way to hide my new preternatural upgrades. Then as quickly as they appeared they disappeared into a thick dense mist that swirled around me with the stray breeze. However, my fangs remained as a sign of what I was…whatever that was.

CHAPTER FIVE

"Hey, babe!" a deep burly voice called out, I turned slowly, like you do in a nightmare when you know the monster is right behind you.

He was big, I don't mean tall, though he was that too, well over six feet, but big also, not really fat but he had weight on him, solid fat like a kind of muscle.

"Would you like to join me and my boys in a little party?" A lecherous smile broke across his homely face and a giggle escaped his lips like a pervert at a magazine rack. There was a scalding wind creeping across my skin like when you open an oven that has been on for a while. I couldn't understand what it was because a minute ago it was a typical cool New York night, in late August.

"Would this party include all of you big boys and lil' ol' me removing articles of clothing," I reply with the sweetest tone. I have a tendency to lean toward being a sarcastic pain in the ass when I'm nervous or confused or angry or pretty much every other mood.

The breeze had died down but my hair flew in streams across my face. I looked at him and noticed that his jacket was billowing like we were in the middle of a storm. But nothing around me seemed to be reacting to the wind and none of his friends seemed to feel it. I realized just then not only was that hot wind coming from him but he was also directing it at me. Every other emotion was pushed away and I was left cold, but not the kind of cold that and extra sweater would fix.

"Hey baby with me there are two ways to party, with a smile on your face or screamin'. And if you play your cards right maybe both, heh heh heh."

I rallied and found my backbone powered by anger. I wrapped that anger around me like a warm blanket. It felt so good and once that anger was wrapped firmly in place that wind that he pushed against me began to die down and his smile wilted around the edges.

He started laughing again as if I had done something to impress him. His condescending

laughter made me want to stab him just to watch
him squirm and because he had scared me, but I
held back the urge. I could see his throat
working while he laughed and I wanted to tear at
it and taste the blood scalding hot down my
throat.

I could remember the feel of the flesh
giving under my teeth it was almost like I could
smell the blood under his skin. It should have
scared me how hard I was working not to kill him
but it didn't. It was becoming increasingly clear
what their intentions were, but they had no idea
what kind of party they were in for.

He walked up so close that a hard thought
would have made our bodies touch. He was trying
to intimidate me with his size. I stopped being
impressed with size years ago. At a hairs
breadth over 5 feet I have been the smallest kid
on the block all my life. Big grizzly here was
wasting his time.

I mean I really tried to compose myself. I
really, really didn't want to hurt them but
sometimes people get hurt. And maybe I do have a
complex about my height; it was the only excuse I
have about what I said next, "It takes all of you
to party with just me," I grabbed his crotch and
continued, "Well, I can see why. There doesn't

seem to be much of a party here." See I told
you I could be a pain in the ass.

Ok, ok maybe I shouldn't have said that and
maybe I did want to hurt them, but I was gonna
walk away, I really was. They had yet to give me
a reason to kill them, until…
WHAAP

He caught me off guard and slapped me to the
ground; the slap was so fast I couldn't see it.
He let me feel the immense strength that he was
capable of. If I had been a regular woman he
would probably have broken my neck. No human
could move the way he did just now. That told me
two things. One: He either knows I'm not human
or doesn't care and two: he is too stupid to
live.

"Bitch!!! Don't nobody talk to me like
that," then he looked around to his friends
laughing and said, "you know I really shouldn't
be callin' these hoes bitches but ya know how I…"
I stopped the sentence before it had a chance to
leave his mouth.

He looked into my eyes as they faded and
began to glow with the same iridescence as the
full moon that hung high in the starless
Manhattan sky. They shine bright like two
captive stars and I noticed that some of his

buddies were shielding their eyes and hissing flashing fangs in their mouths that rivaled mine.

I uttered only two words, "Thank you."

Then I leapt on him and wrapped my legs, firmly, around his back. With my fanged teeth I clutched firmly around his throat. It wasn't until I gave his vocal cords a view of the world, that I could feel the hot liquid rush, pour down my throat like water from a broken dam. I worried at his throat like a dog with a bone.

The blood poured down the front of our bodies, an intimate slickness as warm and lubricious as other things. I kept digging at his throat until I hit some thing solid, bone. Not many animals in nature have bone crushing strength in their jaws. But as I clutched his spine between my teeth I knew that I was among that elite group.

I bore down and felt that solidness give and just like that I crushed his spine with my teeth. As he dropped to the ground, he burst into a pile of dust in my arms. That broke me out of the blood lust momentarily. I coughed through the ash and I looked at the remains of him, thick on my clothes in astonishment.

"WAAH! Whoa-HO! Did you guys see that?!? He…That was…The thing is…He just went POOF! What

the Hell are you people? GAH! I'm probably
breathing him in right now."

They started circling me, their eyes glowing
blood-red and their fangs gleaming like polished
ivory under the full moon. That hot wind smacked
into my body again like a summer afternoon in
Hell. I looked at each one of them and I could
almost see the energy rising off of them. It was
like looking through the heat of a fire.

My own power flared with my rage in response
with a wind so strong you would expect to see
leaves blowing but it didn't seem to affect
anything but the creatures surrounding me. I
finally released all that rage in one wordless
scream.

Their hands went up as if guarding against a
blow. When their hands dropped from guarding
their faces one of them stepped forward, a blade
as long as my forearm appeared in his hand as if
it had materialized from the darkness itself.

He squatted abruptly and answered my
original question in a voice painfully deep like
his throat shouldn't have been able to make that
sound, "We are the ages in flesh. We are older
than mankind. We are why your ancestors huddled
around their fires afraid of the dark. We are
the night. We are Vampires!"

Then he darted towards me. His speed was unreal. It was as if he was a video being played in fast forward, and if I was anything less than what I was I would have been dead before my heart reached its next beat. His speed would have been impressive by any other standard. However, it was only a shadow of what I had done in the jungle. This, I guess, was just not his lucky day, but I must applaud his effort.

I grabbed his arm and the knife, using his own momentum I threw him straight up into the air, and then tossed the knife after him. It spitted his head with a loud *Thunk*. There was a sharp crack like the sound of a whip as the impact of the blade snapped his neck.

From about 20 feet above the ground his head landed first with the blade lodged hilt deep. His body burst into ashes like a spent log in a fire, the blade finally landing on the ground with a rattling clang that was loud in the suddenly silent courtyard.

Everyone froze unable, I think, to absorb the situation that quickly. I think I could have killed them all while they watched, mouths agape, what I just did to their comrade. Then finally as if someone just pressed the play button on a

VCR they rapidly close in on me and once again it's on.

Once again my body moves with deadly ease. I dealt three lethal blows to the hearts of four of the undead. I execute moves that I have never known. An elbow to the creature behind me kills not only him but the one behind him takes a protruding rib to the heart. I kill in deadly earnest with movements nigh-impossible, a truly elegant *Danse Macabre*.

I battled with a bloodlust that I had never experienced. The killing delighted me and the wails were music to my ears. And I know it shouldn't have. I knew in a distant way that I shouldn't be able to kill so easily, that it should bother me. There was a little voice inside my head that told me that this was wrong and that I should find it detestable, that killing so easily and brutally is evil but that voice seemed so far away. I only felt bad that I didn't feel bad. But that didn't deter me from killing those that were trying to kill me.

It was a simple thought process. I was less conflicted than I had ever been. I thought vaguely that this is how wild animals must think. Survival of the fittest. Kill or be killed. But even that was too complicated a thought. Simpler still, survive. And survival means you're alive and everyone else is dead. Like I said, simple.

The last one lurked up on me and I spun and raked his face. With flesh still under my fingernails I delivered fatal strikes to his temples, heart, and throat. He screamed as he left this plane of existence in a ball of flames.

The battle was over. The silence was so complete that the blood rushing in my ears was a deafening roar. Adrenaline at work. As I stood amidst the swirling ash with my blood soaked hair wafting in the wind a rich, melodious voice emanated from the shadows with ominous words that continue to caress my soul, because they were the first words I had ever heard him say.

"And unabashed the Devil stood making his mock of me."

The words floated on a cool wind like an ancient tomb being opened after centuries of dormancy. I wasn't sure if I had imagined the wind, but my skin prickled with gooseflesh. His voice was laced with an Old World accent, Spain maybe or somewhere even older; it was like velvet rubbing the inside of my head. It touched me like no stranger's hands should. He glided towards me.

It appeared as if every step he took was into the shadows like he was using them deliberately. I couldn't see his face beyond the blackness of the hood. I couldn't tell if it was a practiced movement or something else.

He walked like he was restraining a power so immense it made my bones ache, a kind of stalking glide, graceful like he had muscles in places most people didn't. The cloak he wore was so long that the only way I could tell he wasn't hovering was that recoil of force that the earth pushed back into him with every step he took. Even a cat can't beat physics. I was glad, it made him more real somehow, and I could hurt real, dreams were a bit trickier.

His words put me on the defensive. Though my enraged state slowly dissipated it still loomed deep within my chest as if it were burnt coals that only needed a little prodding before the flame would burst out and completely consume you. I would say he finally stepped into the light but that wasn't exactly it. As he removed the hood the shadows peeled away from his face like a snake shedding its skin.

When I could finally see his face he was… was… beautiful. He was like some black angel carved from the night itself. Too pretty to be

called handsome, he had high cheek bones that
looked like they were sculpted with a knife,
silky hair pulled back tight in a complex braid
falling just past his shoulders. I used to call
my hair black but now with his to compare to mine
seemed a poor substitute. It shone under the
light of the moon and gave the illusion that you
could see flashes of color if you looked long
enough.

That gleaming blackness was pulled tight to
the sides of his head it gave the impression of
being short ending with a froth of shoulder
length curls. Being pulled back showed off his
too green eyes to great advantage. They were
like cat's eyes. No human has eyes like that.
The utter paleness of his skin made the contrast
of his hair and eyes that much more startling.

His jaw line was solid, definitively
masculine, ruining any illusion of femininity,
with a dimple in his chin like his maker pressed
his thumb into the clay before it hardened.
Finally there was that look in his eyes, the one
that only men can achieve when their thoughts are
filled with surety about a woman.

He spoke again and it made my chest tight as
well as other things, "Well done, child. You
exhibit a degree of power rarely seen in a

newborn. I hope that you did not take that too personally, *mi amor*. I just needed to be sure."

"Sure of what." For a reason I could not explain the urge to kill wouldn't completely leave, "Who are you? And why do I want to kill you… slowly?"

"Mmm, are you trying to scare me *mija*. I am far too old to be afraid of anything," he paused.

It was as if he'd been holding his breath and finally exhaled. That cool prickling wind changed into a bone chilling blast from the mouth of Dante's ninth circle. I swiped at my arm expecting to feel frost but there was nothing. But then again, it wasn't that kind of cold. His power felt like dying, alone… and he seemed unmoved. He just continued to stand there as he said, "But you are welcomed to try. Before you do so I want you to know that I have killed stronger and smarter creatures than you."

It felt as if the air was growing thick like something you put on your pancakes rather than breathe. My lungs were burning but I had a smartass comment to make and by God I was going to make it, "Soo… let me get this straight. You showed up late when they were giving out all that survival instinct and just decided to pack all the hair gel you could into your bag?"

"And you do not have very much respect for your elders. Has your upbringing been that suspect?"

"What did you just say to me?" I asked slightly wounded.

I lunged at him and he side stepped. I once again slipped effortlessly into that graceful killing dance. My flurry was as powerful as it was useless. It wasn't like he was dodging but he just never seemed to be where I expected him to be. It sounded like there were hundreds of whips cracking but I hit nothing but air. The look on his face was all for amusement, this was a game for him.

I hate when people find my anger amusing. I landed only one hit and that was the only one that instead of dodging he blocked. When the two of us connected he shoved some kind of energy into me. My whole body froze with sensations that were far too… intimate for someone that I just met to illicit. Things low in my body clenched almost painfully tight. It was embarrassing. He countered with lust and had me subdued.

His face held a blank nothingness like a wolf in the forest that you have accidentally snuck up on. It stands frozen. If you attack it will defend itself, if you leave it be it will run. It doesn't matter which just that it is always ready. That look in his face told me that I have already lost. So I let it go. See, even I can be smart sometimes.

"Very good child. You have a sharp mind after all. You have developed power nicely and much quicker than any other that I have seen."

"What?!?! What are you talking about? Let me go, you bastard!" Well that common sense didn't last too long.

"You do, however, need to learn to control that demon rage. That kind of passion needs reins or you will have a very short stay among us."

"Us? Who is us? Who are you? What the Hell is going on here?"

"Hell is exactly what is going on. I have been called many things, but you may call me Vincent and you are a newborn child of darkness. You are a well of hate and bloodlust. Even now you can feel it ebb and swell. It is a part of what you are now. Enjoy it but control it as well."

"What I am? Y-you know what happened to me, what... what I am?" I asked my voice shrinking.

"You are a killer. You are true beauty. You are immortal. And you are extraordinary. Even I feel the pull of your body," the tone of his voice held things for the privacy dark bedrooms.

The last was said with a whisper that made my body convulse with sensations that were sooo not pain, "You, *mama*, are the Succubus."

My voice came breathy as if I had been running, yeah, running, "That's medieval Christian mythology. That's impossible."

"You know what, you are insane. That's what this is. You're crazy, and I'm out of here," my voice sounded almost normal, yay for me.

"Before you go, explain to me the wings, child. Or the men turning into dust. Or even your joy in slaughtering the worthless creatures. Did you do a lot of killing before today?"

"No! That is not possible because I… I died, didn't I? I died and now I'm back. How? Why? And everything, everything that I have seen is horrible. So much pain… I didn't make it did I? This is Hell isn't it? I'm in Hell." No I would not cry, not yet.

Chuckling to himself he laughed, "Do not be so melodramatic *niña*. This is most definitely not the *Inferno*. You are far from that pit. You

are on Earth, and you have been given a glorious
gift, the gift of immortality. But tell me,
child, how? How did this happen? Your kind no
longer exists. There is no one that could have
given you The Breath."

I began talking, quickly, but stumbling on
my words, which made for little more than
incoherent babble, "A-A giant… There was this
temple and… Oh God! Joshua, David… and the
others… then…"

"Calm yourself *mija*. It will be much
simpler if…" He tried to reach out and touch me,
but I instinctively recoiled, "Be still newborn.
I only intend to find out what happened. I would
never harm you."

"*Liar!*" My mind snapped at him. Biting my
tongue was all I could do from blurting that out.
The taste of blood in my mouth was distracting
enough for me to allow him to invade my soul.

He placed one hand over my eyes and one over
my heart. I felt a jolt and everything that
happened in the jungle replayed in my mind in
vivid, gruesome stereo.

My brother, my men, my love, they were all
of them were slain at the hands of a beast. But
there was more, something else that I didn't
remember. After I died, I found myself traveling

down a dimly lit path toward a shining star when a silhouette of a woman appeared.

She began speaking to me, but her words came as inaudible echoes and in a language that I did not understand. But I did catch one thing that her words didn't tell me. She was scared and she was in trouble. Her eyes screamed for help.

All I can remember myself saying was "Don't worry. I'll help you."

Then I was back, looking into Vincent's eyes, he whispered almost to himself a name, *"Morrigan."*

This name held no immediate significance to me but to him it meant something more. His eyes changed, there was a tightness around the corners of his mouth. The changes were slight but noticeable. If I knew him better I'd say he was worried. At the time I couldn't understand what could worry someone like him.

I began to ask, "Who's…" but my thoughts were shattered by the wails of sirens. Apparently we attracted some attention and he changed the subject. *"Permiso, nena,* but I have to go. The sunrise is fast approaching."

"How can you tell?"

"Sniff up, *que linda,* do you smell that intoxicating aroma. It smells like a fresh rainfall, roses, and vanilla all rolled into one. That, *nena*, is the sunrise."

He put the hood of his cloak back on and began to leave, but I stopped him for one last question, "So all that about vampires and the sun is true, but what about me? Will it kill me?"

"As you might have already guessed, you are quite a unique creature. I have never met one like you. I had only heard stories. I could not know what would happen to you in the day, but if I were you I would not test it, best to get inside before that first sun kiss."

"*Liar!*" I don't know why that shot through my head again but something inside told me not to trust him.

He turned around and said, "Hope to see you soon, *mija*," then the cloak dropped to the floor and he was gone.

Seconds after he was gone I picked up the black cloak and put it on to cover my blood soaked clothing. I reached inside one of the pockets and found an envelope with my name on it. It was an invitation to a party at his house the following night.

Just as I began to place the hood over my head an intense light shone into my face and a loud commanding voice with the indelible order of the policeman, "Freeze!"

Well, fuck.

CHAPTER SIX

I turned around and walked leisurely toward
the patrol car with my hands slightly raised, and
two male officers stepped out of the car. This
couple was so mismatched someone must have lost a
bet or something.

The one barking orders was a corn-fed,
chiseled All-American Iowa pretty-boy. He looked
like he should be on the cover of Seventeen or on
one of those WB shows about pretty, white kids
with problems. Dark blond hair, close to a sort
of light brown, cut close to his head, very
professional, I guess it helps with the
authority.

His skin was tanned but being the middle of
Fall I doubt he was tanning on the beach, more
like his family was doing some naughty things
with the dark-skinned help a few generations ago.
His eyes were the color of spring skies and he

would have been handsome but the scornful scowl took away from it. He had every Middle American stereotype working against him complete with the high school jock mentality.

The other was a walking stereotype in his own right, an over-the-hill rotund beat cop. I never really understood what it meant when they said someone was portly until now. He was very round and had, maybe, 3 or 4 inches over me, which made him a short man. He had one of those thick mustaches that men used to wear a generation ago, and it was starting to speckle with grey. He looked like he wanted to be back at the station wolfing down a baker's dozen.

Sigh Now look who's falling into stereotypes, sorry. But he did look like he has seen too many nights and is weary of the streets. It was his turn to play good cop now, I guess, because he began to speak.

"Ma'am, what are you doing out here."

"Standing down and offering submission," I replied, "I wasn't aware that it was illegal now to be ethnic in the ghetto."

"Listen! We don't need any sh—"He reminded me of one of those rookies in the movies that always seems to get himself killed.

"You might want to watch your tongue, before I rip it out," my thoughts pierced his psyche like a laser. There was a sharp sting at the back of his mind and his reaction was noticeable, almost like I had struck him.

"I'm sorry, Miss," he spoke up obviously apologizing for his partner's discourtesy, "we received some reports of a disturbance in the area. Did you see anything? Do you need any assistance?"

You have to admire the false sympathy. He sees me standing in a courtyard full of broken glass and ash covered head to toe with a cloak and he asks now if I need any help. After the interrogation.

But I guess I should be grateful that I had the cloak on because if he caught a glimpse at my clothes stained with other people's blood I would at the very least have guns trained on me again.

Something inside told me to push them, "Yes. Sleep for me sweetie."

Sure enough tubby sat against the car, tilted his hat, and nodded off. Oh and you better believe spunky didn't like that one bit.

He drew his gun quick, fast, and in a hurry, and he seemed upset, more than just a little bit, "What did you do to him?!?!"

I took a step forward, "You might want to worry more about what I'm gonna do to you, puddin' tater."

"What? How did… Don't move! If you take one more step I'm gonna have to put a 9mm hollow point in that pretty little body of yours."

I don't respond well to threats so like a good little girl I took another step, and, if he is anything, he is a man of his word; he did open fire. Three burst shots just like they teach at the Academy. His bullets hit nothing but air, then I took two more steps forward, and he fired another salvo. Those little gnats went screaming into the night never fulfilling their purpose. He couldn't believe what he just witnessed. I tried to imagine what he must be thinking but was suddenly stuck with an utter lack of caring. He turned to run but he tripped over his own feet, his face stopped an inch before kissing concrete. I caught him. I lifted him back to his feet and crushed his gun to scrap.

My voice transformed into something not nearly as pleasant as it was a minute ago, it was less human; it had more of a growl to it, deeper than my voice could ever get on its own, "I'm sorry. Did I pull out my wallet too fast!? Or did I suddenly remove a CD from my pocket without

warning!? Because if I did; I apologize. It is
police like you that always give us the chance to
make the ten o' clock news. Do you know what the
news is going to say tomorrow night? Do you?!?!"

He began to shake with fear. I could smell
the stink of it. It was like the pheromone of
death enticing me to kill him. I knew that his
blood would be hot with it and with that thought
it was over my body was on auto-pilot.

"N-no," his voice cracking, he was at the
edge of tears.

The big pulse on his throat throbbed
quicker; it was almost hypnotizing. Beads of
sweat began to appear like dew on his forehead.
He smelled like food.

"It will open with, Police Officer Nicholas
Andrade, slain last night, is survived by his
wife and 3 month old daughter. This is what you
get for being so ignorant and for pissing me
off."

"N-no… please…"

"Begging, oooo, how I love when they beg.
Oh Nick, please, don't stop."

This wasn't even me talking any more. I've
never been this deliberately vindictive. There
was a little voice at the back of my head trying
to make its way to the front. I couldn't hear

what it was trying to say but I had the feeling that whatever it was it was important. But right now the only words that came out were cruelty at its purest, at its most sadistic.

"H-how do you know so much about me? How did you know what my mom used to call me?"

I had, absolutely, no clue how I suddenly knew all these personal details about him. All I had to do was look into his eyes and I knew all the things that were going through his head.

"Such a nice, tidy uniform," I began to tear at it with my nails, "You keep it so very neat and clean," I made a small scratch across his chest and licked the blood off, "I know everything about you. I know about your wife, Beth, and your daughter Becky. I even know about your best friend who you cheat on your wife with. What's his name, Victor, right? You can't hide anything from Death."

"Wh-What are you?" He began to cry and I licked the tears from his face, salty with fear and the knowledge of his own impending doom.

"Do you believe in vampires, Nick?"

His eyes widened like every story that he has ever heard about demons, Hell, and monsters in the dark has come true.

And it has.

"I-Is that what you are?" he whimpered.

"You'll never know."

I sunk my teeth into his throat and a kind of weird mist...

Ha, kind of weird I say...

...started to rise from his body and absorb into mine. I could feel his heart speed up then it began to slow. He started to pray, The Lord's Prayer, but it was not until his heart skipped its first beat that I realized what I was doing.

That that little voice inside began to scream, "THIS IS WRONG!!!!! STOP!" Vincent was right. I need to control myself. I almost took someone's father away. I dropped him still alive, still breathing, and flew off.

I made it back to my apartment just as the sun began to peak over the horizon. I felt like crying, I needed to think about what just happened, but dawn waits for no one, a beam of sunlight shot through my window and hit me right in the chest. It didn't feel warm. It didn't hurt. It didn't feel like anything, just empty. I looked down to see a big, gaping hole in my chest with mist rising off of me.

I tried to scream but the mist engulfed my body and the last thing I saw was my clothes drop to the floor and I was gone. Passed out again?

Well... Double Fuck!

CHAPTER SEVEN

Darkness, oblivion, abyss, these were the
words I would use to describe what you see after
death. Well, for me it's my second time around.

You ever have soap in your eyes and water in
your ears at the same time?

Imagine that tenfold, a hundredfold, it was
the ultimate sensory deprivation. It was
actually kind of cool, if you're into that sort
of thing.

But just as night fades into day, light
slowly began to penetrate the darkness and colors
returned, and then sounds. Finally, shapes and…
and, I was still in my apartment.

"What a gyp."

Disoriented and lightheaded I started to
pull my clothes back on but I only made it to my
undies because when I picked my shirt up. It was

tacky with drying blood. Large red and brown patches formed a gruesome tie-dye. I couldn't remember what happened or where all that blood came from.

As I looked around my apartment I came closer and closer to the realization that something was wrong. I indeed recognized the place, the same off-white walls that every apartment I have ever seen has, the large windows with vertical blinds, the grey carpet that stopped at the black and white marble tile on the floor of my kitchenette but it was the faces in the pictures, I did not recognize any of the faces in the pictures nor could I make out the face staring back at me in the mirror above my couch.

There were a bunch of thoughts and scattered memories racing through my head. But everything was out of order. I closed my eyes and focused on the most vivid thing. I was killed. That fact hit me like a bullet train.

And… "No."

A sinking feeling settled in the pit of my stomach.

Something was missing.

Something was out of place.

Something…

Someone was gone…

"David?"

I went through the house calling his name. Every room was empty and the entire house was still. It was too silent though; there were no cars, no sirens, and no ambient city noise.

"David where are you?"

My body shivered and dread swept over me. My mind started racing then right as I was about burst I heard something. A nearly inaudible whisper, "Sita…"

"What? Who's there?"

I heard it again, a little louder this time, "Sita…"

My voice now beginning to sound desperate, "Where are you?" This time there was nothing, so I snapped, "ANSWER ME!!!"

"Calm down baby I'm right here."

The voice was so warm and soothing. My heart felt like it was going to swell beyond my chest. I spun around and saw a face that was in pieces the last time I saw it. His hair was curly and dark, his eyes the deepest purest brown I have ever seen. He was a whole foot taller than me so I had to step back so that I wasn't craning my neck to see him. His skin was light against the darkness of his hair and eyes but there was enough natural tan in it that you would have to ask if you wanted to know that his family was of diverse heritage.

"Oh my God, David," I leapt into his arms, "I love you."

"I love you too, babe."

"The last time you said that you made a mess on the floor."

"I know. I'm sorry."

"What happened to us? Why is everything like this?"

"Well we have come to the next path. We died baby. I'm sorry there is no better way to say it but that other life has run its course."

"Dead? I wasn't ready for it to be over. I keep seeing it. I still feel the pain like i-it's burned into my soul and I hate everything because of it. The first thing I did was kill, like I could kill all the pain away. Like I was born for that purpose and what's worse is more than just a part of me enjoyed it. I feel like I'm not even in control of my body anymore. I almost killed a man because he pissed me off. I can still taste the blood in my mouth. What's happened to me?"

"That is a little more complicated. You died but you were caught in the middle of a sort of jail break."

"Jail break?"

"Yea. An ex-demon named Morrigan was trying to escape from Hell and you got caught in the middle."

"Morrigan? Vincent said that name. Who was she?"

"Like you she was a succubus. She died centuries ago; more precisely was killed, by the vampire you met tonight."

"Wait! Just wait! Are you trying to tell me that I am possessed by some demon with a psychotic vampire stalker? This is what you're telling me. You do realize that that sounds complete insane. You really sound touched in the head. How long have you known me? You know I don't believe in any of that; the Devil, demons, boogey men that is all nonsense. It's all just a social construct used to keep the feeble minded populace in check and stem rebellion with the fear of damnation, an opiate for the people. It's not real. It's crazy."

"Crazy like, being murdered by a giant. Crazy like not believing in death. Or maybe its crazy like thinking your actions had no affect on the lives around you. I saw you down in the alley with those vampires and more importantly with the police officers. Think. Did that seem like you? That was bloodlust, you are experiencing it."

"What?"

"Hunger," he said hunger like it should have been capitalized. "Sita, I love you and I hate that I'm the one that was chosen to do this but your current situation is not an accident; it's of your own doing."

"Your soul is a good one. I know that. I wouldn't have fallen in love with you if it were otherwise. However, you were so badly scarred all those years ago that something inside you died, and with that death you stopped caring about life. When that happened you strayed from the flock. You lost your faith and you stopped believing. Whether or not you choose to believe in God, or Satan for that matter, they both still believe in you. And both want you to come home. You gave up on your soul and events were set in motion to wrench it from you. Why do you think Vincent was expecting you? And of all the people that have ever died and moved on why do you think this is happening to you? The world that you built to hide from the pain of loss is gone.

Certain things exist whether you want them to or not. The sooner you come to realize that the better. Morrigan realized this too late and she lost her soul. Ironically she has given you a second chance and in the process she might save herself. You have got to start believing again for both of your sakes. You have to continue where she has fallen. You each have your strengths and you have to help each other otherwise all is lost."

"Laying it on a little thick there, ain't ya Yoda? You had me at Sita I love you. What am I supposed to do?"

In the worst Yoda impression to date he replied, "Well, young Padawan, worry about tomorrow night you must."

"What? What's happening tomorrow night?"

"You don't pay attention to anything do you? You were invited to a party."

"Stop… Pause… Rewind… W, T, and F?! You just told me that that psycho murdered me once already. Why, oh, why do I want to go to his house? For Sports Center Highlights?"

"Well, he doesn't know that you know who he is. He is expecting you to show up. And if you don't show up well he is gonna come looking for you. I don't think you need the gory details beyond that. It's best to keep up appearances for now and trust me he won't try to kill you so soon. He's sorta scared of you. That's why he killed you in the first place. It intrigues him to be afraid so he'll probably keep you alive until he is either sure you are not a threat or sure you are."

"Why is that not comforting?"

"Don't worry you'll be fine. I am here to guide you."

"Fine? The last time you said "fine" I was nearly executed in Mexico for grave robbing," we both smiled recalling that memory.

"Good times, good times. But that's in the past now; you are my charge, and it's up to me to watch over you."

"Well, where were you looking when I was getting jumped by vampires?"

"You looked amazing. You don't need any help with that. Morrigan knows how to handle herself. She will keep your body safe. My job is to keep your souls safe."

"Well what if my body still needs you? Or are you not allowed to do that anymore Mr. Guardian Angel?"

He answered me with a chaste kiss, a kiss that was ten times better than any sex that we have ever had. My knees buckled and he caught me in his arms, "What do you think?"

Our lips hovered over each others and I grabbed the back of his head in that rich thickness of hair and pressed our lips together again so hard that it rode that line of pain that is so close to pleasure that you can't tell the difference. I was still in my bra and panties and my nipples were already tight and pressed against the soft cloth of his t-shirt.

He put his hands under my butt and lifted me up and I wrapped my legs around his waist all this while our mouths explored each other like this was the first time. He carried me over to the bedroom and closed the door with his foot.

My hands were full with that dark hair while I kissed, caressed and explored his face, his lips and neck. He laid me down on the bed slowly then knelt next to me and undid the button on his pants. I stopped him and started with the top.

I slipped the shirt over his head and just looked down at his smooth hairless chest, nicely tanned with dark nipples rigid and stiff I put my mouth over one of them and played with it with my tongue as I undid his pants myself. His boxer briefs that I bought for him were tight enough

that I could see that he was hard and ready
through the thin cloth.

I looked into his eyes and he kiss me as my
bra fell onto the bed. I didn't even notice that
he had removed it. My naked breasts pressed
against his chest as we continued to kiss and he
slowly lay me down and he went down on top of me
our lips never parting.

I could feel him hard pressed against me,
only thin pieces of cloth kept us separated from
each other. He slipped his hands inside my
panties and slid them over my hips and off they
went onto the floor. He put his hand between my
legs and slid a finger inside the fleshy wetness
of my body, and my body tensed and he brought me
with just that, he swallowed my scream in his
mouth.

I didn't realize he had already removed his
underwear until I felt him hard and warm slide
into my body and it brought a small moan from me,
and he swallowed that down too. He drew himself
out of me bringing small helpless sounds from me
until only the very tip of him was still inside
me then he thrust himself inside of me in one
powerful motion.

It made me gasp, and he did it over and over
and over. I couldn't form words or thoughts I

suddenly felt that tightness again and a wave of
pleasure wash over my body and then he turned us
over so that I was on top. I wasn't sure that I
could move after that but I managed to swerve my
hips and when I could finally feel my legs again
I sat up.

Staring into his eyes I lost myself. I fell
into those deep pools and every part of me was on
fire. Nothing else mattered, not life, not
death, not Heaven, or Hell. This was all there
was, this moment. I was falling in love all over
again. "I guess this is what it's like to make
love to an angel."

"Yup, so what do you think?"

"No words, baby, no words."

As we began to climax together mist started
to rise off of my body and we levitated above the
bed. We were art. This was the reason life was
created. Our passion built to its crescendo and
we erupted into an explosion of ecstasy. When it
was all over David was gone and I was alone
standing in the shower watching the pinkish water
and thicker things swirl down the drain.

I was sure that it had to be a dream but it
felt so real. My body was flushed and I was
still tingling. But whatever it was I took it as

a good sign and did what the hallucination told me.

CHAPTER EIGHT

The address that Vincent had given me was a high rise in Midtown. It was postmodern architecture at its best, all sharp angles and shiny everything. Glass and black marble pillars stretched into infinity. It reminded me of my favorite scene in the Matrix but if I remember everyone in the lobby died so it wasn't that comforting.

Even in his little uniform I could tell the doorman wasn't human, neither was the security guard or the elevator operator. At this point I began to wonder if I'd made a big mistake.

The elevator opened at the penthouse and I was greeted by some young… well, young looking, vampire who gave me a wide, toothy grin, his fangs gleaming as if I were his favorite movie star that just showed up, unexpectedly at his house.

His eyes focused to finally see me and his mouth just hung agape. I wore a white evening dress that was low cut and backless. The dress hung down to my ankles but was slit so high that only the most carefully constructed thong would suffice.

If I moved right you could see ankle all the way to hip. I was short but it gave the illusion that my legs went on forever. His stunned silence was all the compliment I needed for the night.

His hair was short, styled with hair gel. It was dark with curls that framed his face, he'd have to shave it to get rid of the curls. Grey eyes peeked out from under long eyelashes that women would kill for.

"*Why is it that men always have prettier eyelashes than women?*"

They were set in a face that that was smooth and perfect and the color of pale honey. His face as a whole was too soft like he would be frozen in pubescent good looks. His body also looked unfinished. Broad shoulders down to narrow hips a high school wrestler's body. He couldn't have been more than nineteen maybe when he died.

He was almost my height give him and inch or two barely. Short for a man, maybe he didn't hit his growth spurt yet and he never would. He wore a deep red silk button-up, so sheer I could see his nipples beneath the fabric.

Sex and blood, the symbolism wasn't lost on me. I wanted to touch it to see if it was as soft as it looked. He had leather pants that off set the red silk nicely.

I flashed him my most innocent smile, and realized that the fangs in my mouth would give me away, so I just walked past him without saying a word. He stood there with a stunned look on his face; obviously he noticed that I'm not just any other girl.

The place smelled like old death, a dry mummified odor, but there was also that musty smell of life. There weren't just vampires in the room.

It looks like they brought some snacks to the party, because that's what a good party guest does. Being dead doesn't change that I guess.

Through the crowd I caught a few stunned faces; through the faces I searched for an enemy, someone ready to step forward and denounce me, but the assassin never came. In the crowd were some familiar faces, some you would never expect and some that were just obvious. Hollywood, politics, religion you name it Vincent definitely attracted the upper crust.

"*Forever the aristocrat.*"

The thought wasn't mine but I agreed. This party was an exhibition of quiet hedonism; think of the Playboy Mansion, but who a lot more pretense and arrogance. That bored me so I lounged on the couch all night like an ornament, unrestrained in my true form. I waited and eavesdropped on conversations trying to pick one out about me. I heard jokes about food, sex, breathing, and other things that vampires found amusing.

Every corner of the room was taken by dance, conversation, feeding or… other things. But no hostile comments, no malicious remarks. Hours past and I witnessed debauchery in excess. Intemperance with wild abandon became ordinary. I actually found myself beginning to relax, which tells you how tainted my soul had become. That all ended when I realized just how far into the abyss I had sunk.

"The feeling is mutual," was the response I gave to a former teen pop queen that MTV had convinced the public into believing had talent, who said that she loved my wings.

"Do you mind if I touch them," she asked.

"No, not at all."

"Mmm, how I envy you," she said, "they make you look so powerful, so beautiful."

"Really," I said with a nauseatingly pretentious tone in my voice.

As she walked away she stepped on my tail, hard, not trying very hard to make it look like an accident. A whimper escaped my lips and she kept going chuckling to her friends. Heat crept up my arms, hot like fire burning to my bones. It was almost painful like a hot wind out of a volcano. But there was no wind in this room. It was coming from inside me. I was doing just fine at suppressing that rage but she pushed me over the edge.

I scanned the room not yet knowing what I was looking for. The room was elegant and dark filled with monsters, some demons some not, but all monsters. I felt like everyone was looking at me, and every time I locked eyes with someone I got a flash of their most recent sins. Murders struck me with terror, rapes washed shame over me making me feel bare naked and exposed, mortified. The pain from all their victims whether great or small hit me in sickening waves until I thought I would breakdown crying.

I closed my eyes when I felt that heat well up behind them. I didn't cry though. No I wouldn't. If their victims could suffer so, the least I could do was avenge them. Did they deserve what I was about to do to them? At the time I thought so, but in retrospect I'm not so sure that was my decision to make.

But if there is one thing I learned from this whole story is that the past can't be changed so I won't dwell on it. I opened my eyes and finally saw the room. Everything was a glamour, none of it real. Velvet and marble, satin and ebony it was all illusion. This room was filled with horrors, nightmares laughing in their decadence. The decision was made I would shine a light and rid the world of these shadows. My efforts were not in vain, I found what I was searching for.

I slowly sauntered across the room with a sultry elegance, so arousing it was a sin worthy of a demon. I let my intent fill me and spill out. I opened myself and the power I left in my wake made all heads turn toward me. I climbed onto a table and they began to cheer like a bunch of drunks at a topless bar. I scanned the room once again looking at each and every face, and finally I asked, "May I have your attention please?"

Then I ripped the velvet shrouds from the wall. The dazzling sunlight poured in, they almost didn't understand what was happening. It wasn't until I smelled the burning flesh that the collective scream started to rise as one sound, a macabre chorus and amidst the screams of agony I heard a woman's voice say, "It's beautiful."

Vampires are dead. They are shells, a pale reflection of what used to be. They are cold blooded killers, a cancer on God's creation. They exist to corrupt. They rape everything that is good about humanity and they revel in it, for that they deserved to die. They don't deserve to be here, but then again neither do I. As I began to disperse I tried to leave something with my essence. A memorial of sorts, I bloomed a rose from the ashes of one of the monsters that I'd just murdered, in hopes that someone will appreciate it for what it tries to be.

Beautiful.

CHAPTER NINE

I regained awareness in my apartment, and sitting in his favorite chair, my love. "David? How did I get back here?" I was still disoriented, but my mind wasn't as clouded as the first time. My vision was edged with this haziness like being drunk but with out the oh so fun dizziness.

With a combination of disdain and concern he said, "You shouldn't have done that."

It was hard to concentrate on the tightness of his words with this atmosphere pressing on me in this unnatural way.

"Done what," I replied, honestly ignorant to what he was referring.

He opened his mouth to say something then seemed to think better of it.

The silence stretched and I realized he was going to answer me when he felt like it. So I thought of a question that he might answer.

I asked, "What is this place? Last time I thought I was in my apartment, but there is something different about it. It doesn't feel real, more like a dream."

"You're not entirely wrong with that observation," he said, "It is a dream in many ways. It's the 'in between' so to speak. It's everywhere, yet no where. It's here and there. This is the place where dreams are born, the place where nightmares can never follow. There is no name for it that would be sufficiently thorough as to explain the exact nature of this place in a way that you or I will ever fully comprehend it; it is simply the place where the soul exists, and it takes the form of a place where you feel most safe. Incidentally that place, for you, happens to be here at your apartment."

"Ah so I am tripping balls, you say."

Then he repeated his earlier statement, "You should not have done that."

"Done what? What are… you… talking… abou…" at that moment what I did rushed into my head. All the pain I just inflicted the look of horror and the agony of guilt hit me all at once. I started to smell the burning flesh, and their screams were like razor blades on my soul. My body folded like I had been struck. Their eyes were wide with pain and surprise, and reflected in it something like betrayal. I was… am one of them how could I cause them such pain. "My… My God," I said voice thick with tears.

"I see you remember now."

"What was that," I asked barely stemming the tide of tears.

"That is penance embodied. Think of it as instant karma. The things that we do that we know are wrong when we are alive can be easily justified or forgotten, pushed far to the back of our minds, but you can't hide from it here, never here. The person standing in front of me right now is the soul of the woman I loved. You are the manifestation of your own goodness and conscience. What you did was commit murder."

"They deserved to die; they were evil."

"Maybe so, but who are you to determine their fate. Some of them were humans that you killed. You set them on fire right along with the vampires, but you knew that. You did not kill them for divine retribution or in self-defense or to protect anyone. You killed them because you lost your temper and for the joy of killing."

"The what?!"

"I am grateful to say that you wouldn't understand that concept but it is a trait of the demon that dwells within you. You cannot lose control because when you do you forfeit your soul and all the good you do will be voided. You have powers given to you by the devil but it is up to you how you use them. Never succumb to the darkness. You are stronger than that. Your destiny is meant for greater things than murdering vampires. You know that guilt that you felt immediately afterwards, that was Morrigan crying out. She is the same as them her existence is as a result of the darkness of chaos and whether you believe it or not so is yours. She knows the horror of perdition and she knows that the path you are taking is the same she took that resulted in her being cast into the pit. Also what you have succeeded in doing was ruining your element of surprise. They will now be after you and that will make it difficult for you to accomplish your mission."

"Mission? What mission? And who is this Morrigan dammit?"

"Sita…" he said then stopped and started over, "I suppose you have the right to know." He paused to take a breath, then he continued, "Everything you are going through right now didn't just come out of nowhere. It's a story that's more than millennia old."

*   *   *

Morrigan was one who as the said it in those days indulged in the pleasures of the flesh. She committed every sin of carnality in The Scripture. She loved sex and couldn't get enough of it.

Sex was her tool, it was her weapon, and it was her vengeance. She began her life as a peasant serf in the French Mediterranean in what in those days was called Gaul. She lived a simple life like most did in her day. But early in her life she was betrayed by her father when he sold her to a brothel. She spent several years being sexually abused until a most unexpected thing happened. She fell in love, but as it turned out a forbidden love.

The son of the Madame took an interest in her as she did him. He promised to take her away from that life but the Madame would not lose her most profitable whore. When her son went against her and took Morrigan in the dead of night to free her from that and marry her she sent bounty hunters to hunt them down.

When they were caught they took pleasure in raping her while he watched then killed him in front of her. That broke her, and she spent the rest of her life breaking any bonds of love that she came across.

There was a reason she was the wealthiest whore in France. She did more than seduce men's bodies, she stole their hearts as well. And when the Madame died she took over the brothel, but she didn't give up her job. She took pleasure in her ability to corrupt men, to eventually destroy all that they were.

She would sleep with anyone who could give her pleasure. She had broken up marriages, corrupted an innumerable amount of couples, and after finally taking all their money leave them broken and wanting. Worst of all she took all of their lives with her disease.

That brutal attack left her with more than just emotional pain. She was dying from syphilis and she knew it. She had grown bitter and vowed to take as many as she could with her. But in lies the paradox of her death. She didn't die from her sickness.

The circumstances of her death were a mystery to all the eyes above and below, only to the Creator was the secret known and He was

unusually keeping her destiny a mystery. She
died in an accident that would be deemed tragic
by all those involved.

A young boy had fallen through some ice and
inexplicably without thought to her own safety or
her hatred for men; she leapt in to save him.
With no regard for her own ailing health she
stayed with him and kept him warm until the
villagers found them but in her weakened state
she succumbed to pneumonia and hypothermia.

She was no more than your age when she died;
young even for those harsh times. In the eyes of
the people she was a heroine but in heaven's eyes
she was a harlot. For her misdeeds against
humanity she was sentenced to carnal congress
with the devil as penance, but the Creator,
though strict, is not blind.

She would not spend eternity in torment;
however, once she was truly repentant she would
be allowed access through the gates of Heaven.
But, Lucifer would have none of that; he made her
into a new kind of demon.

*   *   *

"A succubus," I whispered.

"Yes, *the* Succubus, a lustful demon that feeds off the essence of all living things. Mostly she fed from the libido of men. She would seduce them and then devour their souls and leave them as charred corpses in their beds, burned alive by their own passions. By keeping him in constant supply of unclean souls the Prince of Lies had firmly secured Morrigan's soul to the darkness.

She went on killing this way for a few hundred years. She gained notoriety and infamy. She had many names over the centuries among them Child of Lilith and Bane of Men. Her ruthlessness caught the eye of a vampire as cruel and powerful as she was, Vincent.

It was like Lovecraft, Dante, and Shakespeare sired some blasphemous romantic epic that would make Caligula seem like a mild manic-depressive. They remained lovers for decades, it was a union spawned in Hell. Not only did they feed from humans, but they fed from vampires, and all manner of preternatural denizens, even each other.

They became nearly invincible, and they formed a demonic empire in the Old World. They rose to power by seducing the wealthy and powerful, then finally killing them or bringing them over to the darkness assuming their lands and titles like demonic Lord and Lady. Any attempt that was made against them was always quelled personally in a most pitiless fashion. They were powerful in both the human world and demonic. They had no equals, save each other.

Their rule was absolute until one day Vincent had a vision. He saw the power that Morrigan would someday wield, power that would over shadow his own and that she would use it to eventually kill him. His anger and jealousy manifested in a murderous fury and the last thing she saw was Vincent's rage filled eyes through a fiery haze.

She went straight south, and it hasn't been until now that she's been able to escape the relentless sexual assault of The Proud One himself. However she was hence denied access into the gates of Heaven, and will spend eternity in Hell unless she can fulfill the destiny that was denied to her and you."

"She asked for my help."

"Her life was spent damning men, consuming them and hating them. Only through love and sacrifice can she and by extension you find redemption."

"But we were in love."

"Fate is not without a sense of irony. I am dead my love."

"Fuck fate, we don't believe in destiny or predetermination, remember? We make our own decisions."

"Yes you do, we all do. You could have easily told her no and went on to your final destination. You could have rejected Joshua's offer. I could have chosen not to go with you on that dig. Even Morrigan could have chosen to live in her grief and keep her soul intact. But none of us did."

"The big things are God's domain but it's the little things that we get to decide. It's always the little things. It's the little things that get us through life, and it's the little things that we take most for granted. It's not who lives or dies, or the sun rise or what the big plan is that change the world. It's what we do everyday we wake up. It's who loves us and who we fall in love with. It's that polite smile we give that passing stranger who for all we know was on their way to depression and suicide until you acknowledged their existence. We change the world everyday by just existing. But sometimes, just sometimes, there are things that we must do, things that are beyond our realm of understanding. These are the things that we give back for the gift of our existence and these are the things that justify the grand design and these are the things that we call our destiny."

"But why me David? Why does it have to be me?"

"I think that some time ago a carpenter's son asked the same question and I'll tell you what was told to him... I don't know."

"Not comforting..."

"Wasn't meant to be. Before you leave though, I'll leave you with a bit of advice; do not kill any mortal, innocent or guilty. You can neither pray nor die, but you can feed from the immortals. You'll need to. You should kill the creatures of the night only for that reason and in defense of yourself and others. I know how this all sounds but you read The Book you know how He is about His rules. But be careful you have now gone behind the veil and you will now see that at which dogs howl in the dark, and that at which cats prick up their ears after midnight."

Then he placed his hand over my belly and his eyes locked onto mine. Finally he said, "And above all else make sure you protect this most precious life you carry."

"What, what did you say?! Life?! What life?! David..."

CHAPTER TEN

My words were merely whispers in the night for I was back. I was back at the scene… a shiver went through me. The floor and walls were charred like there was a five alarm fire. There was dust and among that bones. Vampires don't leave bones behind when they die. The thought didn't have time to sink in because there was a sound.

Footsteps …they'll kill me if I didn't get out of there. Someone was coming; I picked up my dress and flew out the window before my heart reached its next beat.

As I flew over the city I hoped that no one would look up and see me naked flying over them; who knows what they would think. After what seemed like the show-up-to-school-naked dream that always lasted an eternity I landed on the roof of my building with a clatter that sounded

like horses galloping. Then I felt it. The
twinge up my spine that told me that one of them
was near. This one was strong and his power felt
like a hot wave from a blast furnace.

I turned around and one of them was
following me. The heat that engulfed the power
told me that he was a little miffed. Angry… well
who could blame him I just cooked all of his
friends. It was the doorman from Vincent's
house. He shouldn't be too difficult to
dispatch, I thought. Well, considering he was
flying after me without wings maybe that would be
a little premature.

He touched down onto the roof and shouted,
"Newborn! You have not been a part of this world
very long and I am here to shuffle you off this
immortal coil. You have broken one of our most
inviolable laws. You can kill the humans, maim
them, rape them, and torture them all you like;
Hell that's just plain fun. But you never, never
bite the hand that feeds you. Your master's word
is above law. It is divine mandate. You
murdered nearly his entire court. Do you know
the sentence for apostasy?"

"I can guess," I replied, as I put the dress
on, I just wouldn't feel comfortable fighting

naked, "but, uh, I didn't get your name at the party."

The smugness nearly dripped from him, grinning he replied, "Humph, my name is Angel, but you…"

"Ri-ight, Angel," I interrupted, "Um, Angel?"

He frowned at me, "What!"

"Shut *Up!* Are you going to try to kill me or not? Because I'm getting bored."

His carefully constructed hubris began to fade as he let his eyes fill with the monster that swam just beneath the surface, "Let's see that confidence when I'm picking bits of you from my teeth."

He lunged at me snarling like a rabid wolf, his speed was remarkable. He matched me move for move, as we fought across my roof we made windows implode with the impact of our blows. As fast as we were moving I was biding my time for him to make a mistake no doubt he was waiting for the same thing.

The next thing that happened was inevitable, his fist connected with my face. The force knocked me from my feet and split the concrete of the rooftop. We both took a full minute to react to the new situation, but I spent that entire

minute trying figure out how brutal to be. My
eyes faded to a pale blue, my mouth began to
water, and instinct replaced reason.

"You're going to regret that the rest of
your life… both seconds of it."

"Now who can't stop talking newbo…"

My fist clenched so tight that I knew there
would be crescent moon shaped wounds in my palm
from my nails digging in. The swing cut off his
words before they could pass his lips. I felt
the bones of his face give under the impact of
the blow. He lay on the ground bleeding all over
himself. His nose was flattened and blood
drained from it like a pinched off faucet.
Bloody tears ran down his face as he cried.

His broken teeth had shredded his tongue so
he slobbered his words out, "Please… don't…"

I gave him a passionate kiss and licked the
blood from the ruin of his mouth. I moved from
his mouth to his throat intending to end him but
as I prepared to bite him he used the last of his
strength to put his knee into my stomach.

He still had enough strength to double me
over. All the air rushed out of me and I
couldn't maintain my feet. Independently of my
wishes my knees made the decision to buckle

sending me unceremoniously to all fours,
sucking in loud gasps of air.

He ran to the edge of the roof and spoke
again, mouth already beginning to heal, "I'll…
be… seeing… you."

Then he leapt over the side.

*   *   *

As I sit in a familiar coffee shop I listen
to the sirens and watch the lights pass by
responding to the three alarm fire coming from my
apartment, a fire that I started. What's
happening to me?

Blood, the sight of it used to bother me.
Death was something that I couldn't process. I
ignored its existence. But now… now it's all
that I know. I can still feel blood on my hands
and taste it in my mouth. I can smell death,
feel it.

I am death.

This is a nightmare that I'm in. As I sat
there and tried to absorb what was happening and
what I had become I… don't want to know. Its
foul and repulsive, I am a monster and all I know
is evil. I have lost people, people that I love

and I can't even cry for them. Something is wrong with me.

A child? What child? We don't have a child, we can't. "Dead people can't have children." But even as I sit here and say it to myself out loud I know what he said is true. I don't know how but I'm pregnant. I'm a demon and I got pregnant by my dead fiancé. It... It doesn't make sense.

I continued to sit and think and try to decide what to do next but my mind would only circle around one thing.

"I wonder if I started screaming right now would they give me my own room at Bellevue or would I have to share?"

CHAPTER ELEVEN

Driving down a dark road… the car goes into
a skid… it swerves then flies off of a bridge
into a lake. I was no longer in the car, but I
was the one that lodged the brick onto the
ignition pedal. My car, it's the last remnant of
a dead life that will *not* be forgotten.

The smell of an approaching storm filled my
nostrils, and a memory came to my mind. It was a
good memory, a memory that was not mine. The man
she loved, truly loved, who was her first…
everything. The rain begins to fall and I see
him. His eyes lock on to mine through the sheets
of rain as he takes me in his arms. Another
feeling swept over my body, in complete contrast
to the fits of rage that I had been experiencing.
It was a more sensual feeling, very tranquil,
bordering on erotic.

It was now raining... pouring. I was no longer in control of my actions. I began to remove my clothes and let the feelings sweep me away. I was anything but an exhibitionist but I gave into the compulsion to shower in the grace of God. It felt right, pure, like I was becoming brand new.

I have never been a big fan of religion and over the years my spirituality has admittedly waned, but after everything that has happened I needed to feel connected; I needed some help; I needed someone to hold me up and give me the strength to carry on. And I felt that now. I felt as if I was now being imbued with strength.

Not the strength to kill, like I've been doing, something else. At the risk of sounding like too cliché the only way that I can describe it is a Strength of Spirit. It was overwhelming and I began to cry. After all this time, after everything that has happened I can finally cry. I shed tears now for all those that have died because of me and I shed tears now for the life that grows inside of me.

I don't want my child to be raised in a world with such evil in it. But it seems as if I don't exactly have a choice now. The experience of my death, of my rebirth, and now of this beauty that I am feeling has all worked to strengthen my resolve. My resolve to make all the evil that is a threat to my baby pay for what it will try to do and my resolve to bring Morrigan and myself to the Holy Land.

After all the tears have been shed, and everything had been washed away all there was left was the carnal lust and delight of the breeze across my flesh and the fat drops of rain hitting my shoulders, rolling down, and dripping off my rigidly stiff nipples.

I feel her presence in my mind sad, lonely, and proud. The knowledge of the ages fills my thoughts. The Succubus is a creature of pleasure; she knows the true essence of sensuality. She is lust incarnate, hedonism embodied, and sexuality manifested. She is the siren of men, their song, their sovereign.

I could feel something well up inside me, something that wanted out, that same animal that paced its cage in the jungle, something primal, something fierce. The heat starts at my face then travels down my back. Part of it erupts and when it does my wings explode from me, but it's not over. The heat continues down and my tail follows, finally my toes fuse and lock into my hooves. My heart speeds up it feels like it

wants to break through my chest. Finally it
erupts in one last burst of emotion as I scream.

I am Passion!

All of this combined with Mother Nature's
caresses were so eerily arousing that I was
paralyzed with pleasure. I lay on the grass
exposed in my full diabolical glory, a demon
writhing in ecstasy. The scene was something
right out of an old fairy tale or a Heavy Metal
album cover, your preference.

Then the rains had ceased, the tears had
passed, and a ride was not more than ten miles
down the road. While I waited I pulled my
clothes back on and fully regained my composure
with the exception of my nipples still stubbornly
hard beneath the cooling fabric of my shirt as a
reminder of what had just occurred.

I succeeded in hitching a ride from a state-
trooper named Welby Montalvo. I know that before
he opens his mouth. His eyes were a deep blue
like midnight skies. I had never seen eyes like
that and they were kind but there is a deep well
of pain beneath them. He smiled though, but the
smiled never reached his eyes, almost a fake
smile but I knew better so I so didn't hold it
against him. As I watched the world speed by I

replayed all the events of the past few days in
my head.

"Miss uh, Miss…" His voice seemed a million
miles away, "Miss where are you headed…"

I pretended not to hear the question,
without looking at him, almost to no one I asked,
"What's the nearest town?"

"Well that'd be where I'm headed, Vahalla.
Is that where you're…" The car stopped abruptly.
I looked right at him, and he apologized as he
was staring disdainfully through the windshield.
I looked and to my horror it was group of
vampires, lead by that one that I fought on my
roof top, what was his name… Angel.

Everything will be ok if we just don't
panic. "Don't stop! Drive through them," I
yelled at him, and grabbed his arm so tight I
could have popped his muscles.

"Ahh…" He winced.

Ok so… I panicked.

"Calm down Miss, don't worry, I'll handle
this," he replied.

"No! You don't understand! They're not
human!"

"What?!" I may have said too much.
"Anyway, I'm going to call for backup."

I sat there anxiously; if he knew what I did he would know that unless he was calling Buffy the Vampire Slayer his actions were in vain. But before he could put the call through one of them smashed the window and pulled Welby through. His speed and strength surprised even me, he was immensely faster than I was; my eyes didn't even register his movements.

He pulled Welby through the window before I had the chance to grab him; he pulled him over the broken glass smearing the door with blood. The other came over to the passenger side and tried to grab me.

Angel tried to warn him, "Rudy don't do it!"

But he was too late, his hand crashed through the window. He tried to capitalize on my vulnerable position; I was bent over trying to pull Welby back into the car and in no position to defend myself. At least that's what he must have thought. But the moment that I felt his clammy emaciated hand cop a feel my eyes widened and I turned and caught him in my piercing azure gaze, eyes aglow.

"Bad boy," I grabbed his wrist, back kicked him in the chin, and then yanked him in the car.

The car rocked back and forth, there we animalistic sounds and I was enjoying myself.

This looked like a very suggestive situation from the outside, but that collapsed quickly when finally reverberating through the country side, his agonizing scream, "MY EAR!! LOOK WHAT THAT BITCH DID TO MY EAR!!!"

I mean I did rip his ear in half but I still don't like being called names so I broke his arm as we exited the car and twisted it into the most excruciating position possible, hoping that his pain would convince them to let Welby go.

They had him on the ground ready to crack him like a wish bone. Why am I always inflicting pain on others? Why can't I stop? I didn't want to be captured but I also just didn't want them to keep hurting him. I didn't know what to do.

"You're a dumbass Rudy. I told you she was strong," said Angel. He continued, "Sita, he can heal from those wounds. But it won't be so easy for your little man here. They are so terribly weak. So, why don't you just let him go and come with us?"

"No," was the only response that I could just barely muster. Following that Angel stomped Welby's head, cracking the pavement and causing the patrol car siren to bleep. Then he tossed him against the car with authority, almost through the door. He appeared to be unconscious;

at least that's what I'd hoped. He became
indignant, and raised his voice, "Now that
wouldn't have been necessary if you would have
just cooperated. I can't promise you that I
didn't kill him. Just let Rudy go and come with
us, Sita."

It never stops. Everyone that I meet; I
only bring them pain.

"Why? He didn't do anything," my voice was
starting to falter.

"Just come with us! And I promise the only
one that will be hurt is you."

I couldn't stand it anymore, enraged I just
snapped, "Why can't you people just leave me
ALONE!!!" Following my outburst I snapped Rudy's
head all the way around shattering every bone in
his neck. For him light fades to darkness, and
his soul is condemned to Hell. All that remains
is a pile of smoldering ash.

And I reiterate, "Leave me alone!"

With that they prepare to rush me when
suddenly a sound explodes and rings through the
night and Angel's friend suddenly comes down with
a splitting headache. The blood splatters on
Angel's face as the gunshot echoes through the
cool night air.

Wielding the smoking gun, Welby defiantly declares, "Damn vampires."

With his muscle incapacitated Angel suddenly loses his nerve and fled parting with a statement that I'm sure wasn't in his best interest, "To Hell with Vincent. Next time it'll be just you and me, and I'll kill you myself."

He disappeared into the night leaving his comrade with only half a face desperately trying to reinsert his eye. I walked over to him with intent; I grabbed him by his collar and dragged him off the road into the tall grass that surrounded us so that Welby wouldn't have to witness what I was going to do to him.

It's never a good idea to kill someone in front of a cop, even if they are already dead. The weather was appropriate, beautifully clear, dark skies, with a small chilling breeze that sent goose bumps up my skin.

I pinned him to the ground and asked, "What does Vincent want from me?"

Choking on his own blood he sputtered, "I-I don't know…" then screamed as I ripped out his partially reforming eye and crushed it.

"You've lost a lot of blood," I told him, "it looks like it's getting difficult for you to recover."

"All he said was to capture you alive because he loves the way you taste."

"Animal! Auggh!" I cried as I swiped his face with my nails. Streaks of dark flesh went flying into the night.

"Please don't kill me…" he shrilled, "I was just following orders."

"It's ok, it's ok, it's not going to hurt," I said with a very soothing tone in my voice.

"I-I don't want to die…"

Then softly I said with finality, "I know, I know. But then you should have never been born."

Her words coming out of my mouth.

I sunk my teeth into his throat and I let the sweet viscous fluid drain down into me. Hot with fear, his blood was different from the human's it was stronger and more potent. My muscles tightened, and my heart sped up. Heat crept over my skin, but it was a good heat something like passion and a warm bubble bath. I could actually feel myself getting stronger. It was without description. After draining Angel's lackey I rushed over to Welby to see how badly hurt he was, but was met with a drawn gun.

"You're one of them, aren't you?

I was surprised that he even knew that creatures like us existed. I didn't believe in

any of this until I woke up one day and killed
a giant. I wanted to explain but I realized that
no explanation that I could give would be
reasonable so I simply answered, "No…"

"Then what are you, because you're not human
and you are obviously dangerous."

I couldn't help but wonder how he could be
so sure. He lost the little trust that he did
have in me that I was just any other girl, but as
long as I didn't make any threatening moves he
wouldn't shoot me, not after I saved his life,
his conscience wouldn't allow it.

Since becoming what I am I've noticed that I
have been able to read the story of someone's
life through the windows of their eyes, and his
eyes tell an epic, of interminable agony and
guilt, but through all that pain he is gentle
like a rippling pond. That pained me even more
since I felt as if I was taking advantage of his
kindness when I lied to him.

"I'm here to protect you," I managed to
stutter.

His blues widened, an expression of surprise
if I ever saw one, "From what Miss… uh, Miss…"

"Sita. My name is Sita."

"Sita," he said as he lowered his gun.

"I'm here to protect you from those… those…"

"Vampires. Yea I know they exist. And maybe it's just me but I don't think that they were looking for me," he said.

"Maybe…" I replied lowering my voice, embarrassed at being caught in my obvious lie.

"Listen if you're straight with me I can help you. You saved my life so regardless of what you may be it's not completely bad. And if it pisses off the vampires I'm all for it."

"Th-Thank you… um, but before anything we have to get you to the hospital."

"No it's alright, I'll be fine," he insisted.

"Look at the concrete over there. You see that? Your head did that, not to mention slamming into the side of the car. You need some serious medical attention. I can overpower you if I have to."

"I believe you but…" before he could finish his sentence I was kneeling next to him checking out his head. He jumped, startled by my speed, but after taking a look at his head I was a little more than startled myself. It was unbelievable how much damage there was… not.

"That's… That's impossi…"

"Looks like we both are a little more than special. But this is a conversation for later this ground is getting a little cold," he chuckled.

I looked in his eyes and all I could see was pain. His mind was so clouded with it that nothing else but his kindness could seep through. He tried to get up but failed.

"Welby! You're hurt take it easy."

He stopped and looked at me and asked, "H- How did you know my name?"

When he was finally able to stand under his own power I could finally see that he was tall at least six feet. And he was handsome in that masculine, brawny kind of way. He had partially forming stubble on his face and his hair was wavy light brown probably to go with his eyes but black in the night sky.

He was built like an athlete; I guess you have to be to be a cop. I just knew under that uniform there would be abs solid as body armor. Officer Tubby he was not.

Heat crept up my face and I realized that I was blushing at the same time that I realized that I had been staring and not answering his question.

"Yea I… uh… have certain talents, but if you aren't gonna answer me then let me at least help

you up and I'll drive; you are probably
concussed. I don't want you passing out at the
wheel."

Yea that's right I'd choose bossy over
embarrassment anytime.

We made it to town and it was so quiet and
still, so different from The City, *"I can stay
here, they'll never find me,"* I thought.

"My wife Vanessa is probably sleep; I'll
introduce you in the morning. You can stay in
the guest room until then."

I couldn't shake the feeling that he was
being too nice to me, especially since I lied to
him, but I didn't sense any sinister intentions,
only guilt and pain. I think being dead has made
me more cynical.

"Thank you for your hospitality. I really
appreciate it, but can I ask you one thing?"

"Shoot."

"How did you know what those guys were? And
that I wasn't human?"

"I have my talents too, and don't worry we
wont disturb you I know you need your rest to
take care of that baby."

After that last remark he went to his
bedroom and shut the door, but not before smiling
a closed grin and saying, "G'night Sita."

CHAPTER TWELVE

A little startled by his very specific observation I scanned the room and noticed something hanging over the bed.

A crucifix.

And out loud I said, "If I know my folklore correctly this can mean only one thing can come next…"

It started to glow I gasped then screamed. It glowed bright like burning magnesium, a small captive star. I shielded my eyes as I fell through a vortex of anguish.

Now I know why demons hate crosses. It punishes us for inhabiting the earth when we belong in Hell. I felt as if I were being crucified. I felt the nails being driven through my wrists and feet, the heavy iron bolts shattering bone and snapping the muscles in my extremities. I felt the thorny crown jabbing

into my scalp; blood was running down my face,
and bloody tears dripped from my chin. I was
seeing through His eyes and feeling His pain. I
could look down and see the Romans laughing and
my mother weeping. His misery was torturous.

My body was weighing down on my lungs,
squeezing them like a vise. I was being
suffocated by my own body weight. Then I felt
the dull edge of a spear blade jabbed into my
side. It was like being impaled with a baseball
bat.

My blood flowed freely all shiny and red in
the morning light of spring. My body seized in a
bone and muscle snapping paroxysm as the pain
came to a climax, but just as I was about to die
I wasn't on the cross anymore. I was lying on
the grassy field from earlier naked in the rain.

The sudden switch from the extremes of pain
to the extremes of pleasure was a unique
sensation. This vision was different from what I
had experienced on the side of the road. I was
recalling things that I didn't remember happening
the first time.

This time there was an angel, my angel,
David. He descended from heaven in a brilliant
light moving between the rain drops as if they
weren't real and baptized me with the rain. It

burned an invisible cross into my forehead, and
I had become a child of the Lord again. I shed a
single black tear, to wash away my evil. Both
our souls had been consecrated, though our body
was still a demon.

Then I opened my eyes and David was kneeling
over me as I lay on my back in my unburned living
room.

"Sita, Sita are you alright? You appeared
here unconscious."

That can't be good. I tried to say it out
loud, but it came out, "Thhmm kammm shhhh ffoo."

"What happened?"

My thoughts were hazy, so I responded
weakly, "D-David? Blessed… Rain… My angel."

I reach up to touch his face but darkness
ate at the world then lost consciousness again.

My eyes popped open and I sat up with a jolt
sitting next to me was a woman and shining into
the room was the sunlight. It made her perfect,
jet black hair sparkle. It was straight and hung
below her shoulders. She was the prettiest women
I had ever seen.

Her eyes slightly wide with surprise but
gentle. They were light brown almost amber. Her
lips were full and naturally pouting. Her skin
was tanned but looked creamy white against the

darkness of her hair. She was full-chested
though not enough to be considered heavy but
enough to help her thin frame fill out the dress
she was wearing with the floral prints.

It was something more suited to spring than
this chilly autumn that we were currently in but
it looked sexy on her even to me. She had scars
in a white mound, old scars, on her wrist and
collarbone. But they more added to her beauty
than detracted from it. They made her more real.

"What's going on? Where am I?"

"Calm down," she had a soothing voice,
almost motherly, that floated over you and made
her assurance even more believable, "You are
safe."

Was everything a dream? Was she right that
every thing was okay and that I was safe? Please
tell me all of those monsters and all of that
death was just a nightmare.

"I know that you are not human."

Well, that answers that.

"And I know that you are not evil, at least
not completely. But we did take the cross out of
here, you will be ok now."

She was so kind, just like her husband.

It must have shown on my face because she
said, "You looked puzzled are you ok?"

What I am confused about is how can I still be here? It's daytime. "Did you say you know I'm not human?"

She smiled at me the way a mother would smile at her child doing something cute, "Well... the glowing cross and you writhing in pain from its light was a give away." Then her eyes dropped, embarrassed, I think. "I almost killed you."

My heart sped up, slightly and my eyes narrowed then she continued, "But Welby explained so we wrapped up all the crosses in the house and put them away. You apparently aren't a vampire but I haven't seen anyone react the way you did to a blessed cross that wasn't a vampire. But here you are sitting in sunlight but unable to bear the light of the cross."

It was my turn to look embarrassed, "Umm..."

She saved me from having to explain, "Oh I am so sorry. How ungrateful of me. You saved my husband's life and here I am interrogating you. You've done good by us all I can do is offer you a home for as long as you need. My name is Vanessa by the way."

"Sita," I said a little wary, "how is it you know about things like me?"

I catch her eye and see that she's tempted to invite me to church but she thinks to herself how dumb that would sound so instead she asks me to have breakfast with her. It's weird I have only been apart from humanity for a short time but it already feels awkward interacting with them. I can sense the eternity within me and I know how fleeting all of this is but I accept her invitation.

I sit across from this woman and can taste her mortality like bile on the back of my tongue. She is like a candle burning from both ends, but at the same time that candle is brilliant and shining. I used to be like her. I long to be like her. I am jealous of her mortality and as she speaks I hear none of what she is saying. I want it all back. She is a good person.

"*I used to be good.*"

"Huh?" she asked.

"Did I say that out loud?" My voice came out vulnerable.

Damn it.

I will not cry.

She looked at me with the one thing I couldn't stand in that moment… sympathy. That was it. I broke down and cried. She held me in her arms and I cried. The more I tried to stop

the more and harder the tears came. I sobbed
like I could cry all the pain out, like I could
cry everything normal again.

And beneath all the crying I could her
Vanessa repeat over and over again, "You are
good, Sita. You are good."

CHAPTER THIRTEEN

She never once treats me different. I sense
her unease about have a strange woman in her
house but she never lets it show. If things were
different we could have been friends. But all I
can think about is last night and when that will
happen again.

I think to myself, *"When will I ruin her
life?"*

Days passed and nights; weeks and months
fall off the calendar. I blew up like a blimp
and never once did I disperse in the sunlight. I
lived here with them. I worked in Vanessa's
flower shop. I never talk about what happened to
me or where I come from or even what I am. And
they never push. I try to forget. I try to deny
what I am, and what my child could be. I try to
ignore the fact that I am being hunted, by
vampires. I try and I try, but you know what

they say to try is to fail because just when I begin to feel like everything can be okay…

One night close to the end of my pregnancy I dream, something I have not done since I was alive. This dream is not a mere dream but a portent. I am in my apartment, and was met by two surprised, relieved, and most of all loving eyes; standing before me was David. He practically flew across the room and grabbed me and held me close to himself. "Thank God! You're alright."

"What's going on David? How did I get back here? It's been months and I haven't disbursed in the daylight and haven't seen you."

"The sunlight has not affected you because of the baby. He's not a demon so his purity has kept you tied to earth. The reason we are together now is because he has begun to dream. Demons can't dream, but it is because of our child that I can visit you now."

"Our baby isn't a demon?" I ask with a combination of comfort and puzzlement.

"No."

"So he's an angel?"

"No."

"Then what could he be?"

"He's a baby."

"What?"

"He is a child that needs to be loved and cared for. It doesn't matter what the nature of his birth or his parents. He is innocent. There are those out there that seek to pervert that innocence and there are some that seek to snuff it out entirely. You are his mother and as such it is your responsibility to protect him. That is all that matters. And when the time comes he will decided which way he will go because that is his right so given by the Lord."

"Okay, but what if I'm not strong enough."

"You are."

"But…"

"You are his mother. That is strength enough. Nothing will harm him because you will not allow it."

"You're just saying that cause you love me," I said trying to hide the blush that crept up my face under the intensity of his gaze.

He smiled at me as if I had done something too cute or silly for words then mercifully he changed the subject, "Yeah, well, there is something else. The last night I saw you it was only for a minute and you were out of it. You were mumbling gibberish. Something happened to you, something bad. What was it?"

"Something did happen, but it was far from bad. I saw you. I saw what you did. I thought I felt your presence in the rain. It was as if you were moving between the rain drops. You came down and consecrated my souls. You made us good again. I don't know how to describe it so I just wept. I knew you were there but why couldn't I see you when it was really happening?"

"Sometimes when it rains… that is when the heavens open and the angels are allowed to play. I saw you there in the rain. So I touched you. I took the darkness from your soul and made you once again how you were intended, pure. I made it so that that evil could never penetrate your heart again, and as long as you fulfill your destiny then we will be together again in Heaven. Corporeal beings are usually blinded to the divine, so when we wish to make our presence known we do so via unusual, generally impossible phenomena or as the term has been coined, miracles. Devils can not cry. They have no emotions, no conscience, no will, they are nihilistic killers, they have no souls, but you have two. You feel, you hurt, you cry, you are beautiful."

My eyes are turned down and I want to cry now but I don't let the tears come out, I opened

my mouth and only allowed one thing to come out
because I didn't trust my voice, "Why?"

"Why what?"

"Why me? Can you answer that David? Why
me," after all this time I let myself ask, "Why
the hell does God care so much about me now? He
took everything from me and I have never given
anything back to Him. He stole my life before I
had one, He took my father, then he took my
Joshua, then He took you. Now I'm a demon. Why
does He care about me now that I am unclean? Why
should He care," tears began streaming down my
face and I screamed toward the heavens, not
speaking to David any more, if I ever was, "Why
do you care now, huh? Why do you care!?"

David grabbed hold of me and held me close.
I could feel his warmth as he tried to consol me,
"We're close enough now. I think he might have
heard you." I let myself sink into his warmth
and be comforted, but it didn't last long.

Suddenly there was a sharp pain in my
abdomen and lower things. I gasped for air as I
dropped to my knees. "David… David…"

"It's alright Sita. Don't worry. It's just
the baby. The baby is coming."

"Th-the baby… is… coming? David the baby is
coming."

I began to scream, then I heard a voice say, "Yes the baby *is* coming. You'll be alright, just push… push." My scream reverberated throughout the countryside as I gave birth. It was the worst pain that I had ever experienced, and it was centrally located in one section of my body.

"Push," she ordered, "Push!"

"I'm trying! Gimme a break, I never tried pushing a turkey through a keyhole before." With one last eruption of pain I hear the sound that I had awaited for what seemed like an eternity, but was probably only a few minutes. My baby's crying. The whole room was aglow with a celestial calm that could only be described as without description. I was filled with a euphoric warmth as if David was right beside me holding my hand, which he probably was.

"He's beautiful," Vanessa finally said.

"*He?*"

"Yep, you are now the mother of a healthy baby boy. Do you have a name for him?"

I was literally intoxicated with the love that I felt for my son, "My son…" I said, "I love the sound of that." I looked into his big brown eyes and almost lost myself just like in his fathers. He looked into my eyes and fell asleep.

"He loves you already," Welby said.

"Come on Welby let's let the mother and son have their rest," his wife said. She stood and her hips and butt betrayed her ethnicity and let me know that that perpetual perfect tan of hers was natural.

"You're right, but one more thing," he added, "Sita?"

"Hmm?"

"*Do* you have a name for him?"

As I looked at the tiny person sleeping in my arms I immediately know who this person is, only one name would suffice, "Nicco. His name is Nicco"

"That's a real nice name, where did you get it?"

"It was my father's."

"That's nice, Welby let's go! It's almost time," she said as she exited the room.

"Okay, see you in a few days Sita."

Later on that night Vanessa came in to check on us. "Are you alright? Do you need anything?"

Even after all this time I was still surprised at her generosity, both of them, "I really have to thank you for your hospitality. I have lived with you for months, and you never once treated me as anything other than a person

even though you know I'm not, not to be
ungrateful, but why?"

"To tell you the truth," she hesitated, "at
first I really didn't want you to be here. We
didn't know who or what you are, and I have had
enough of monsters in dark. No you're not human,
but you are a person. Welby told me what you
did, how you saved him and I realized that you
are not one of those monsters out there. You are
like my husband, caught in the dark but separate
from it. Because of that I really didn't have a
choice but to help."

"I believe I owe you a thank you," I
replied, truly touched by what she said.

"No you really don't; you saved my husband's
life. You do not owe me anything."

"They would have killed us both. There is
something else about that night that I never told
you. They beat him... bad. It was an attack that
would have killed most people, also he knew I was
pregnant before even a doctor could tell, and he
feels different. His aura creeps up my skin
sometimes but it isn't like the vampires. It is
like this electric warmth, I don't know how to
describe other than alive, very much alive. Your
husband, he's different. He's... He's not human
either is he?"

"You… You're very perceptive. He is a descendant of Lykaon… a werewolf. Those senses are residual abilities that he possesses in his human form."

"A-A werewolf? That would explain the pain…"

"Pain? What do you mean?"

"His eyes. His eyes told a story of pain. When I first met him his eyes told me that his blind generosity and kindness are atonement for a deeper pain, a pain so deep that I couldn't see through it."

"Wait. Are you telling me that you can read minds? What… What are you…"

Before I could say anything else our conversation was broken by Nicco's crying. "He's hungry," she said, "I'll go get you a towel so you can feed him. I'll be right back."

"Thank you Vanessa."

She wasn't gone for more than a minute before I heard the sound of breaking glass. "Are you ok in there," I shouted. But she didn't answer so I went to check on her. As I got up my knees buckled and I almost toppled over. The combination of lying in bed for so long and just giving birth took a toll on my equilibrium. When

I entered the living room I halted so suddenly
that my feet slipped from under me.

They found me.

CHAPTER FOURTEEN

After all this time, they finally found me. Two vampires had Vanessa pinned to the floor, about to do God knows what to her.

"What the Hell are you doing here! Let go of her," I declared.

Then one of them stood, tall, lanky. But I knew that those spindly arms could bench press a car so I wasn't fooled. He wore an ankle length dirty brown coat. His hair was in messy disarray, but despite his disheveled appearance he had a shape to his face and cut to his jaw that was handsome under all the dirt.

He spoke, "We're here for the child…"

That being the last thing that I expected my eyes widened with horror, just at the prospect of even letting them touch my baby. His words made, almost frighteningly, no sense.

"How could they know about Nicco," I thought.

"I th-thought Vincent wanted me," I stuttered.

The second one barely stood in a crouch. He wore a dark red skull cap so I couldn't tell if he was bald or his hair was just shaved very close to the sides. The cap was wet with something, shiny. There was a red stream running down his face.

"It couldn't be," I thought.

Blood, the cap was soaked in blood, still flowing as if the cap itself had its own heartbeat.

Even crouched his stillness was remarkable, like the way snakes can get when they were about to attack. His eyes were yellow with slit pupils; no human had eyes like that; which also meant that he couldn't be a vampire. He was something else entirely. Vanessa struggled against him but just like his eyes suggested his snake like muscle coiled around her like steel.

A Red Cap, a goblin, the knowledge wasn't mine but it was enough for me to appreciate how much danger we were in.

He finally spoke with a serpentine rhythm,
"Hhhe wantsss the bothhh of you, but hhhe will
get you himsssself."

I tried to remain as tough as I could, from
the floor, but I began to realize that something
was taken from me when David came to me in the
rain.

"If you let her go right now I promise to
kill you quickly." My voice came out steady,
points for me.

Then the vampire laughed and said, "Look at
this one, has she got a pair or what? You can
have this bitch, that one is mine."

He started walking across the room toward me
and continued talking, "You obviously have no
idea who we are, do you? Don't be mistaken,
Love, if I wanted I could kill you before your
heart takes its next beat."

I stood up and my legs didn't shake, another
point for me and I replied, "You just look like
another dumb vampire to me. And you don't scare
me. So leave us alone and get the hell out of
here."

"Ooo…" he said, "I'm loving you more and
more keep talking. How does a little one like
you know anything about vampires?"

I walked right up to his face and said, "You really are an idiot. They sent you in here without knowing who you were dealing with and you didn't even bother to ask. Heh… you are going to die."

I began to feel a familiar electric warmth but this time it was more… it was more biting like a perpetual static shock and the warmth was like a midday breeze in the heart of summer. I could tell that I wasn't the only one that felt it. I didn't see him move but his hand was suddenly wrapped around my throat. His grip wasn't crushing but he let me know the potential was there.

"What is that Bitch? What are you doing?"

I laughed again, "You are such a moron."

There was a short pause, and then something exploded from the basement and dragged him in, I covered my eyes to protect them from debris so I didn't see what it was, but screams of terror and the ripping and tearing of flesh followed the next few seconds, then a hellish bellow. Vanessa began to laugh, her doggy was hungry and she knew it. A dead calm filled the house, and then it was shattered by another burst from the floor.

All I could see was a large ball of hair; it was as large as a brown bear. It stood nearly

seven feet tall. Its legs were bent oddly at
the knee more canine than human. Its tail tapped
against the floor with an audible thud. And its
arms were massive like gorilla arms but ended in
claws like shiny black daggers. It was very
Claude Rains but without the pants and
unmistakably male. The wolf-man's jaws were long
and filled with fangs stained scarlet, and its
pure white fur was speckled ever so slightly with
crimson flecks.

He was crouched on his haunches and growled,
a low rumbling sound that raised both our
hackles. His muscles moved like liquid steel
under the fur steadying him on one hand while the
other held something bloody and solid. I stared
hard at it but my mind wouldn't wrap around what
the object could be. It was protecting me from
having to know, but I kept staring and I realized
what it was. It was the other vampire's heart.
His long, fang-filled, snout ripped into it then
he swallowed it whole.

The whole picture sent ripples up my spine,
but soon I realized that I was safe, because when
it looked at me something in its eyes told me so,
something intelligent, something decidedly human.
It was Welby. The goblin released Vanessa and
attempted to fend off Welby's assault, but it was

survival of the fittest and Welby was without a
doubt more fit. His movements were graceful and
unnaturally quick. It was like watching a video
in fast forward. He slithered through the air
with a boneless grace much like his totem
suggested.

But as quick as he was Welby's speed
immensely over shadowed his. The swipe of one
claw seemed to take up the entire room. I felt
the motion more than I saw it. When my mind
caught up with what my eyes were seeing all I
could make out was the creature dropping to his
knees minus a head. I couldn't even see it
happen. Incredible seemed insufficient, golly
gee-whiz lacked a certain dignity, so I just went
with stunned silence.

Welby relished in his victory with a long
howl, a shrill, deep-chested sound that sent a
primitive fear through my body and shook the
walls with its resonant song. He is Alpha and
any natural wolf would be shamed in his presence.

The sudden quiet after was cacophonous.
Small mewling sounds began to fill the void and
the wind came seconds later, like breath from a
tomb. A red line drew itself across Welby's
body, stark against his alabaster coat. A small
drop of blood had landed on Nicco's face, and ran

down his cheek staining the plush blanket that
I'd wrapped him in. Welby winced then turned to
look me right in the eye. His eyes spoke to me
as bloody tears welled up in them, but only shed
a single crimson droplet as if saying, *"I'm sorry
that I failed you."*

He grimaced then opened his mouth as if to
speak when a sharp yelp shot from his mouth and
pierced my heart like dismal lightening. There
was a wet popping and tearing sound before he
fell in two pieces staining the carpet. Vanessa
screamed as Welby's blood crept across the floor
to a figure sitting on the couch.

"Vincent," I said unable to contain my
revulsion.

He sat on the couch legs out stretched and
comfortable. And at that moment I hated him more
than anything. How dare he be so comfortable
after what he just did. He had a midnight blue
silk shirt with frilly lace on it; opened showing
his hairless smooth chest. White like carved
ivory. It should have looked feminine but it
didn't something about him made it, utterly,
masculine. His boots went all the way up his
legs with straps holding them in place. They
looked like velvet but softer. Only the top of

his black leather pants were visible as they sunk down into the boots.

He spoke and his voice held none of that sensuality that it had had the first time I heard it. It was just a voice, something normal, mundane, completely without emotion like he was reading a grocery list, but it made it that much more profane because of what had just happened.

"While 'round me barked the mad and hungry dogs as he laughed in his gaiety…" his words felt like razors on my soul.

I gasped when I felt the liquid warmth trickling down the side of my face. I touched it and came away with blood.

Did he really just cut me with his voice?

"Well, that's a hell of a thing," I said.

"Pity really such a waste of lycan blood."

"You? You did this," I barely choked out. I saw it with my own eyes but I couldn't make myself believe that he was capable of it. It was too frightening for words. I couldn't even make myself cry for Welby; all I could think was, "B- But h-how…"

"You'd be surprised at how frail a werewolf's body is, my fingers went through him like you move through air," he said laughing.

Then he gave me a look, smug, enjoying how much he frightens me.

Damn him.

"But I d-didn't even see you." I was still unable to absorb the reality of the situation.

He stood up and indignantly shouted, "DIDN'T?! Try could not, child. You still do not get it do you? It has been over ninety decades and while you've been rotting in The Pit I've been living here, in this lush place," he paused letting his voice trail making places low in my body tight.

"Stop it," I whispered.

"Did you say something, *nena*?"

"Stop doing that," my voice had that low tight sound that happens when you don't know what you will do if you don't hold onto it, "No matter what you can make your voice do to my body, you repulse me."

He licked his lips smiling at me but thankfully he stopped and when he started speaking again it was just a voice.

"As you wish, Sita. All these centuries I've been getting stronger," he continued, "You truly do not understand how special you are, do you?"

"What is so special about me that you had to destroy innocent lives? You had no right!"

"Innocent? You are so naïve child. That werewolf has killed more people in a single day than you have the entire time you have been a child of night. Which I must admit is impressive, but his human form was weak. His suffering was odious. You think he didn't want that? I gave him a gift. He welcomed the release."

"What?! You're a liar! Why would anyone want to die??"

"You don't believe me, *mi amor*? Just ask his wife. She resents you because you just did something that her own husband took away from her."

I looked at Vanessa to gauge her reaction, and she couldn't even look me in the eye.

"Her silence should tell it all. As for wanting you; there's an ancient proverb from the dawn of the light, and when it comes to us it holds infinitely true. Think Sita, Morrigan will tell you."

I let myself see. I saw people enthralled. I saw lovers everywhere I walked through them on Vincent's arm. They were everywhere in corners, on tables, in the middle of the floor. Every

part of the castle was filled with indulgence.
But these people were not normal. Something was
off and I realized that they weren't people.
They were more and less than human. They were
everything but. They were vampires, and
lycanthropes, and fey. And we were their lords.
We would choose a lucky set and we would drain
them until there was nothing left and they would
be grateful.

Then it hit me what he wanted. "Me… you
want to drain me! You bastard," my skin flushed
and my heart sped, my anger overshadowing my
fear, "I wish you would try."

"You know what they say about wishing and
how careful you should be. You are not like we,
the lowly dead. You consume more than blood you
consume the spirit as well. All those centuries
of feeding from the most powerful among us has
made your essence a truly awesome thing indeed.
If I had known the depth of your power centuries
ago I would not have burned that bridge," he
smiled, laughing at his own morbid joke, "I would
not have spent all this time learning the secret
of absorbing the power of my prey. But now I
have been granted a second change, *mi amor*."

"You're deluded if you think I will let you
use me to increase your power base."

"Of course not, *nena*, no one let's me do anything. I do because I can. Before I show you how futile it is to resist me it is a curious thing that you have given birth to a child. A new trick, eh? The dead cannot give life. How is it that you have come to possess such a gift?"

"I had sex," I replied, too tired to play anymore.

The tightness around his eyes showed me something I wouldn't have noticed had he not shown his hand. He was afraid, probably a smart thing considering the implications of the existence of a child parented by a demon and an angel. Truth is I didn't know how to explain it even if I did understand how it worked but I just felt the urge to push him. Petty and vindictive I know but he's earned it.

"Do not toy with me, *nina*! What man short of God himself can impregnate a demon?"

I gave him my answer without words, the look in my eyes sufficed.

His eyes widened as if I told him the moon was falling from the sky, "No! That's not possible! Why would He impregnate a lowly demon whore? Unless… No!" He ranted on, and began laughing, nervously, that turgid mask cracking even further, "You have no idea what that baby is, do you? Of course you don't. *Tú eres una niña tonta.* That child is the most dangerous being in existence."

"Dangerous," I blurted out in disbelief, "Dangerous to who?"

"Dangerous to existence as we know it. However…"

I watched the thought coalesce. It played across his face. Then he looked me in the eyes and he grinned at what he knew my only reaction would be.

"I don't care how strong you are. I know what you are thinking and if you try I will kill you."

And he was correct.

He paused for a second to gauge my eyes. My conviction was there but my ability wasn't and he knew that. I stood up desperately hoping my demonic rage that caused men and monster to cower so easily all that time ago would come to me now that I desperately needed it. I searched for that well, that staticky place in me that allowed me to be the monster that I was to once again consume me. But it was absent. But I guess I had known all along that something would have to be sacrificed for my soul to once again be that beatific thing that it was meant to be.

He advanced on me and I took one step back but no further. I realized that he was in a whole other league. I never had a chance. I had no power against him, and there was nothing that I could do to stop him from killing Nicco so a small stream made its way down my cheek. When he saw my tear he smiled and with one finger took it from my cheek and touched it to his tongue.

"No need to waste tears my dark angel; there will be no pain. I swear it."

He walked right up to me and took Nicco from my arms and all I could do was release a hoarse whisper, "Don't… please…" I said with tears caught in my throat, as he continued to smile that most saintly smile; the smile that Lucifer wore as he offered the fruit to Eve.

He held Nicco with such tenderness, but the look in his eyes made me sick. The nail on his pinkie extended to more that double its original length and it was razor sharp, gleaming and black as onyx.

He gently ran it down Nicco's face, paying careful attention as to not cut him. All I could do was stand there and watch, my hands shaking with terror.

He held his nail to Nicco's throat and moments before he would end the life of my newborn, Nicco who had been silent until now began to cry. Then the floor began to shake and moaning echoed throughout the house; a disturbing sound as if the very angels of heaven wept. Vincent looked at me in awe, jaw agape, shock shattering any smugness he had left. I obliged the same expression in returned.

The next thing that happened was truly remarkable; the moaning grew louder and then Vincent's hands burst into white flames that emanated a tranquil blue glow.

"AAH! *Madre de Dio!*" Vincent cried as he dropped my baby.

I dove with all the speed I could muster and caught him before he hit the floor.

Vincent's face was wrenched with agony, but I watched him rebuild his arrogance before he finally said, "The story is told by the most ancient Djeli that 'The Most High and his second will wage a great war against one another. And all that is will descend into Pandemonium. Death will litter the plains of Heaven and Earth. Man, woman, and child will lay strewn stretching into eternity and the Avatar will come forth and it will be ended.' He is the Avatar, the second one in twenty centuries. His existence means the end for all we know. I WILL NOT SUFFER OBLIVION!!!"

With those last words there was no shimmer
or flash I was just staring into empty air,
dazed, as if I had lost time somewhere. I
dropped to my knees and just looked at my baby.

A tear drop of blood had run down and dried
from the corner of his left eye, and a pure,
clear tear ran from his right. I didn't know
what to make of that so I just left it alone.

CHAPTER FIFTEEN

I kissed him and then crawled over to Vanessa. When I sat down next to her she recoiled and couldn't take her eyes off of Nicco.

"Don't be frightened," I said softly, "Vanessa look at me." She slowly forced herself to look me in the eyes and I asked her, "Is it true? What Vincent said about Welby, is it true?"

She lifted her shirt and across her abdomen was a matching scar to the ones on her wrist and collarbone, a claw mark. It looked as if she had been mauled. I touched it and flashes of Welby in his beast form attacking her and going on a killing spree flashed through my mind, hundreds of men, women, and children mutilated.

"Oh my God… all those people," my eyes welled up.

"He and I grew up together. Best friends when we were young, high school sweet hearts, and then in college. We were literally in love all of our lives. One night we were on a date in the city. It was late at night and he wanted to walk through the city. Manhattan is so beautiful at night, there aren't as many people out so you really get to see everything ya' know?"

She smiled recalling the memory,

*   *   *

"Well we got up by Central Park and there was this guy, you know a bum. He was sleeping on the ground but it was too cold. Welby wanted to get him to go to a shelter or something. So he goes up to the guy and he helps him up but the guy was crazy. He started yelling at us telling us to get away. He was saying how it was dangerous and that we should just leave. But Welby...

He wouldn't leave the guy there. I told him that we should have just gone but he wanted to help the guy and just as he was about to come around something snatched him into the bushes. We could hear him screaming and there were sounds.

I had never heard any animal sound like that. It was horrifying. Welby yelled at me to

run. I was just so scared that I just kept
going. I ran and ran and just as I was about to
make it out to the street it tackled me to the
ground.

I tried to scream but it knocked all the
wind out of me. I could feel its hot rancid
breath on the back of my neck. I began to cry
and just when I thought it was over Welby hit it.
It turned its attention off of me and attacked
him. They fought for not more than a minute
before the police showed up and scared it away.
They never did catch the thing but it didn't
leave empty handed. It tore a chunk out of Welby
so big that he was dead before the paramedics
even showed up at the scene. But they went
through the motions anyway. They rushed him to
the emergency room where the doctors pronounced
him dead.

For months I mourned him until I heard about
the string of murders that they had been having
in Boston. They all appeared to be mysterious
attacks by some wild animal. The worst of which
was a whole movie theater full of people
slaughtered by this creature.

I drove to Boston because I knew. I knew
what it was and how to kill it, but I wasn't
strong enough. I got a shot off but I just

grazed it, I woke up in the hospital and there he was sitting there, sitting there like he had never died.

He told me what happened to him and that he tried to control it. I told him that no matter what I loved him and I always would, and that there was nothing that we couldn't face together. And since then as long as I was by his side he never lost control that bad ever again. When the time comes we would just lock him in the basement and no one would ever know.

He dedicated the rest of his life to protecting people that couldn't protect themselves," she paused, vainly trying to stem the tide of tears, then said, "You know… of all the people that he had maimed and murdered, you would think that he wouldn't be able to remember every single one. Their faces torment him in his waking hours and in his dreams. But his worst tormentor is his own child that never existed and never would because of the beast inside him. He never forgave himself for it, and he thought that I never would either. But there was nothing to forgive; I never blamed him, I loved him."

"I'm sorry," I replied, "that is where all the pain comes from. It's his story; his life was suffering."

Changing to a less painful topic, with a trembling voice Vanessa asked, "I-It's true, isn't it?"

"What?"

"What that vampire said about Nicco."

"I don't know. All I know is that he is the only good that I have ever done, the only thing I have ever given to the world. His father, David, told me that I needed to fulfill my destiny if I was ever truly to find absolution, and I just know that Nicco is my destiny. But it is not over. I need to tell you in case all this goes the way I think it will…"

I broke everything down. I told her about my father, about my brother, and my David. I told her about the Guardian's Temple. I even told her about Morrigan. Just hearing it all out loud I had to laugh. The both of us, we just laughed and laughed. I know how it sounds, but it felt good, just you know, to laugh.

After the moment I finally said, "I need to ask something of you. That vampire that was here his name is Vincent, the most powerful vampire in existence, damn near invincible or at least he thinks so. And he is right now the only person outside of you and me that know about Nicco."

"Don't tell me you plan to go against him. Do you really think that you are capable of that? His presence is just enough to make you go insane with fear. You couldn't even move. You're supposed to be this all powerful Demoness and you stood there and let him take your child from your arms to kill him. You will be killed."

"That may very well be a possibility. More than likely I won't be returning from this battle, but as all eyes in Heaven as my witness he will no longer be a threat. So, having said that, I would like you to take care of my son, to raise him to be the man that he is destined to be, a man like your Welby was."

A tear came down her face, "I have always dreamt… I never blamed Welby for what happened but since I was a child I imagined how my life would be, but you know what they say 'While we plan, God laughs'. Our lives are not something that we can plan. I thought I had reasonable expectations, but when I was injured I lost my faith. My plan wasn't good enough for God. He wanted to test my strength. He made my husband an animal, me sterile, and then He takes my husband away from me. Well I'm not that strong! I don't know anyone who is.

Well I didn't, until I met you, someone
who I thought was just here to torment me, a
demon under my roof bearing a child. I wanted to
hate you. But I couldn't, you are so good, so
strong, and then this, you ask me to do this,"
She began to cry again, "Of course I will. I
will love and cherish his life just as if I were
his mother. I love you Sita, I really do.
You're the best friend I've ever had."

I hugged her as the sunshine peaked through
the window, "Thank you…" The sun pierced me and
mist engulfed my entire body and I was gone…

When I finally regained awareness I was
standing in my apartment where David was
faithfully awaiting my return. His face broke
into a wide grin, and I couldn't help but beam
back at him. I ran over to him and jumped in his
lap, and gave him a long deep kiss. We sat in
that embrace for what seemed like hours until I
eventually asked, "Can I beat Vincent?"

"Beat Vincent?" He asked stunned, "No time
to beat around the bush, huh? Why would you even
challenge him?"

"Because he is the only threat left to
Nicco."

"Sita our son is the Avatar of Light. He is
going to lead countless people to salvation.

Hell will send many threats to destroy him.
Vincent is just the beginning. Lucifer will send
many assassins, there will even be an Avatar of
the Dark, but as powerful as they will be Nicco
will never be alone. He will lead an army. Two-
thirds of the stars in the sky will be behind
him. He is loved by everyone in Heaven. He has
strength untold, but as powerful as his mother is
she does not have the strength to defeat Vincent,
the Vampire Sovereign."

"So are you telling me that there is no way
I can defeat him?"

"Are you prepared to go to war? Because
this is the inevitable outcome of challenging
Vincent. Sita you know death, you know pain, and
you know violence, but you know nothing of war.
War is Hope dismembered, grinning at its limbs in
its lap. It is Decency raped to death. War is
Honor wrapped in insanity giving birth to
destruction. War is not the occupation of death;
it is the antithesis of life. It is you alone
against Vincent's Black Court. If you pursue
this you will die, and if you die you will go to
Hell."

"You are asking me if I am going to
sacrifice both of my immortal souls for the
finite life of my child. Am I willing to risk

eternal damnation for his fleeting happiness and safety? Wouldn't you?"

His eyes lowered and his mouth cracked into a grin, "In a heartbeat."

The room started to get hazy indicating that I was on my way back. "I love you Sita."

"Let's make some war."

CHAPTER SIXTEEN

With those last words I was back with his voice echoing through my ears. I found Vanessa feeding Nicco, "Vanessa, I can't take too long because they can come back at anytime, but I just want to hold my baby one last time," As she handed me Nicco I whispered, "Thank you."

That 'thank you' held so many unspoken things, she wisely did not ask and I resisted the urge to say more. What do you say to someone who you've taken so much from and that person asks nothing from you in return? I did not dare stare into her eyes for too long because I just didn't want to know what was on her mind. The raw emotion in them was too much to bear.

I kissed Nicco on his forehead and said my last words to him, "There is a place between asleep and awake; it's the place where you still

remember dreaming. That is where I'll always
love you and that is where I'll always be."

He fell asleep in my arms and my tear
stained his blanket. He was happy and safe at
that moment and if it takes my life and souls I
will keep it that way…
…for now.

Back in the city it was raining. I landed
on a roof top deep in Harlem. Then I felt it.
That electric warmth that told me that someone
around me had power.

"Jesus Tap-dancing Christ! How do you
people always know!"

I turned and found myself nearly surrounded
by growling werewolves in human form, wearing
gang colors. I'll let you guess which ones.

"You guys don't think it's a little obvious
that of all the gangs in New York you work for a
vampire?"

One of them howled and the rest answered;
sounds coming out of throats never meant to make
them. The first one leapt for my throat with no
warning. I used his momentum and grabbed his
shoulders put my foot in his stomach and push
with all I had. It was a perfectly executed Judo
throw just like Welby taught me.

He went sailing over the side with a howl that was cut abruptly. The sirens were already wailing through the night.

They began moving in practiced formation designed no doubt for hunting. The movements were unnaturally swift. All I saw was red and black blurs cut across my vision. Some of them shifted forms others maintained their human shape. I tried to make it to the ledge and one of them blocked my path in a man-wolf for similar to Welby's but black as jet. I think I surprised him when I speared him in the gut taking us both over the side.

I spread my wings and felt a sudden and intense pain as he shredded the membrane of one of my wings with his claws. He slammed into the ground a few feet from his buddy and I managed to glide safely to ground on an abandoned side street.

When I touched down my wings disappeared and I was left with an incredibly deep gouge in my left shoulder. I could hear the howls pierce the night and eclipse the inferior sound of the police sirens. I made it to the 5th Avenue before my vision started to fade from blood loss, when I could feel something else hunting me. This one was nothing like I have felt before. It wasn't

so much a presence as an absence of presence.
It was like whatever it was could drain reality
itself and make everything feel false, like a two
dimensional picture.

The street lights behind me started to
flicker and then go out. Then the ones in front
of me followed. I ran across the street into the
brightly lit restaurant. The people inside
didn't appear to affected by the absolute
darkness outside. They didn't even look up from
their burgers. Then I heard a voice, male I
think.

"Come outside. The mortals can not pierce
this glamour, they cannot help you against the
Wyld Hunt."

I let Morrigan tell me what was going on and
it hit me. I went to the condiment stand picked
up a packed of salt and sprinkled it in front of
the door. The glamour faded and I could see a
shape standing just outside the door. I pulled
my knife made of steel and bone that I retrieved
from the jungle and stabbed it through the glass
right into the figures heart. He spit blood onto
the cracked glass door.

"H-How…? I am Gabriel Woden of the Wyld
Hunt! How could you…?" He gurgled.

"Salt… Cold Iron… Meh, I just don't believe in fairies."

The glamour disappeared and everything went back to normal. The people in the restaurant gasped and stared at me as if I had just appeared out of thin air. I left before any questions stirred and continued east down 125th street.

Just after passing the empty Apollo Theater I slammed into a smell. It was like leaving your, air-conditioned, house on a hot summer day just a wall of musk. But this was definitely not the musk of summer. It was a vile odor like blood, lots of blood and meat, the smell of a slaughterhouse but unclean. Behind the smell of raw meat was bile and the sickly sweet smell of perforated bowels and vomit. Meat, blood, shit, and terror, this was the smell of murder.

I followed the stench to an abandoned building on Park Avenue. There was a chain lying on the ground in front of the door, broken and gnarled as if someone had been chewing on it. There was power on the threshold of the building that my instincts told me should not be there.

"Well then, since you went through all this trouble to set up a trap I shouldn't leave you hanging. That would be rude after all."

The moment I stepped over the threshold I was swarmed by flies and ankle deep in mangled flesh and blood that hadn't been there before.

"Ewww… that's just nasty."

Come on, it really was disgusting.

"Such insolence child," the voice was so painfully deep it sent vibrations through my bones, "these are the remains of every warrior that I have ever slain. They were fools also and you will join them for I am…"

"Yea, yea big and scary, what are you some kind of Orc or something? Well, I never did finish that book."

In the darkness two shiny yellow orbs blinked at me like two Cat's Eye gems, near what I would assume is the ceiling. Another giant… crap!

His yell was thunderous and shook the walls and a blade came out of the darkness larger than my entire body. My arm moved on its own and stopped the blade dead. The force sent small fissures outward across the floor and up the walls.

"What! How? No one as ever stopped at strike from Tyrfing. What are you?"

"Pissed off!"

I wrenched the sword from his hand flipped
it and shoved it in between those two shining
orbs. Blood sprayed from the darkness across my
face and I pulled him toward me, sword lodged
firmly in his skull. His face was strange,
incomplete somehow. If there had been a nose the
sword had taken care of that. His mouth was too
wide for his face as if it bisected his entire
head. It hung agape and was filled with a myriad
of sharpened teeth. His tongue lolled out and
blood pour from his throat.

With one last groan the light in his eyes
faded and he was ended. The power that held the
place together started to fade and the walls and
floor quaked. The bodies on the floor
disappeared and the darkness was less apparent.
I ran out of the door and the building collapsed
no longer able to maintain structural integrity.

"Well that was um... I don't even have words
for what that was."

I opened my mouth to give it one last try
and... "No. Just turn around, Sita, and walk
away."

CHAPTER SEVENTEEN

I was walking down the empty Manhattan
streets; the only creatures out were the
vagrants, the drug dealers, and the occasional
car. And it's been hours since I was attacked by
werewolves, vampires, fairies or trolls.

Yea I know, right? A troll, New York has
everything. Between you and me I'm waiting for a
dragon.

The lightning shot across the sky and the
thunder rolled through the clouds, angry at the
world. Soon after I passed a cop car the streets
became eerily quiet. Suddenly, I became aware of
another pursuer. This tingle up my spine was a
familiar one.

I smiled, "Finally..."

He had been following me for a few blocks.
So without warning I began to duck around corners
and dash in and out of alleys. Nothing human

should have been able to keep up. But his speed matched mine.

"*It begins.*"

No matter where I went he was still behind me.

I made it to Wagner Projects in East Harlem, where I had my first encounter with vampires, seemed appropriate. I found an ambush spot and waited for him to pass, but he never did. I turned around and he was right there behind me, then the lightning exploded and I jumped startled by the whole theatrics of it. I grabbed him by the raincoat closed my fist tight enough to draw blood.

His hood covered his face, and I shouted angrily, "What the Hell do you want?"

My voice was steady, yay for me.

An old tired voice came from under the hood, it held sorrow like a thick fog and it was so weary it sapped my energy just hearing it. "I just wanted to see if you were who I think you are."

"And who am I old man?" The coat went limp in my hands, the old man was gone and my name rang throughout the alley in a more familiar voice, "Sitaaaaa….." followed by deranged laughter.

I immediately recognized the voice,
"Angel. Angel," I screamed, "show yourself you
little bastard!"

"Up here Sitaaa…" He said in a sing song
voice, like a teasing little kid.

I looked up and to my amazement he was
standing, horizontally, on the side of the
building. He pulled his hood off. His eyes were
different. They were wide showing too much
white, the pretty grey that they used to be
faded, to a pale ashen color. All you could
really see was a black pin point floating in a
sea of shining white, almost glowing. His hair
was slick and shiny with rain water. His fangs
glistened brilliant white.

He didn't have to say any thing and I could
tell he had changed. I don't know what Vincent
had been doing to him all this time but he as
definitely become more psychotic.

"Hmm, Sita," he said.

Then he scurried up the side of the building
like a spider and disappeared into the darkness
of the brick canopy. I dug into the side of the
building with my nails and climbed to the roof,
but when I got there I was alone.

As soon as the thought entered my head I
felt it. It was like a swarm of bees flying over

me. Thousands of loud and fearful wings were beating against my skin, the fear of being stung by them all once but the pain never coming. I started to panic.

Deep slow breaths help me concentrate on reality. It was just loud and chaotic and nerve racking. But there were no bees. There was nothing up there but me and him. I couldn't see him but he was here. There was no other source for this deranged energy that filled the air.

"Where are you? Show yourself you *coward!*"

Then his voice came from the shadows. It was abrasive and hot; I felt like my skin was being rubbed off by sand paper. I touched it and expected to be bleeding but of course I wasn't, it was just a voice. He wasn't as good as his master.

"That was real clever, burning your house and disappearing into the 'burbs," but by the time that I looked in that direction he was gone and I was struck down.

"But that's okay. I enjoyed the down time. It gave me the chance to get stronger. Don't tell Vincent but I figured it out."

I was on the ground before the pain came.

"OOOHOO Boy!!! The wonders I've seen. The carnage, the glorious carnage. It was beautiful Sita."

The source of his voice kept changing. "You've gotten faster since the last time we fought, Angel."

Secretly I was worried because he had gotten so fast that I couldn't even see him, also I couldn't keep taking hits like that. Each blow was a Mack Truck between the eyes.

"Because I've figured out the secret Sita," he said, "I know the secret to gaining real power. 'He who eateth of the forbidden fruit shalt be enlightened'.

"Do you know what that means? As fun as it is, it is not the wholesale slaughter of those worthless cattle down there in the street. It tells us to sin, the one true sin, betrayal. No other sin stings more than betrayal. Feed from true evil. Feed from our own kind. Hmph, 'Never murder your own.' I was so naïve. I have killed and devoured so many vampires in the past few months that I am stronger than Vincent," He giggled giddily, "not just their blood Sita but their souls too.

"This is the only true power, chaos. And it makes sense. We are immortal. Why should we

obey; why should we be decent? You know what
makes mortals decent? Fear. Only those who
reject fear and embrace their destiny become
powerful, and that is what I've done. I mean
look at me. I'm immortal. What should I be
afraid of?"

The shadows he was hiding behind peeled away
like a stage curtain and there he stood, no
longer sporting the clean cut, post adolescent
look. He wore a dirty brown trench coat with a
rain canvas. Hair in long waves was heavy from
the rain, hanging in front of his face in long
bangs. His skin had a sickly pallor and his eyes
peered out from under his hair making him look
more feral, like the true predator he is.

I was glad his rant gave me time to get used
to his power. I had a mission and if this was
going to stop me then I didn't deserve to go to
heaven. I looked him right in the eye and told
him exactly what to fear, "Me."

His tone and expression changed from
arrogance to fury and he yelled, "No!"

His power flared and the bees rose up again
this time stinging. The pain was intense but it
didn't matter because he was going to die. He
charged again, then time seemed to slow down, and
he was frozen in space. I closed my eyes but I

could still see him. My enmity focused my mind
to the point that I didn't even need eyes to see.

Everything else was gone but he was still
there. I used this opportunity to my advantage.
I spun out of the way. I opened my eyes and
something invisible to me crashed into the air
conditioner on the other sided of the roof.

He dashed again without a moment's
hesitation. This time I side stepped and fully
extended my arm; he collided with it with the
concussive force of a stick of dynamite. His
larynx was crushed and his body hung limply from
my arm, then I slammed him to the roof. I
slammed him so hard that it snapped his spine and
small fissures spread out in all directions at
once.

Surprisingly he was still coherent enough to
choke out small words, "H-How? I-I'm…"

"You're nothing! Insignificant, little
child I don't have time for you. The question
isn't how, it's where…" I yelled making my voice
harsh, cutting, "…Where is Vincent?!"

It took long enough but he finally choked it
out. Behind his eyes he repeated over and over,
*"Don't kill me. I want to live; I'm immortal. I
DON'T WANT TO DIE!!!"*

"I squeezed his neck and leaned in close to his trembling ear lobe and whispered, "Then you should have never been born."

His eyes widened as I sunk my teeth into his tender, flattened windpipe. His blood flooded down my throat. A cool wind swam across my skin, but as cool as my skin felt my blood was that hot. It was like magma coursing through my veins. The power in his blood was enormous, and as I consumed the last pint he shriveled up to a living skeleton. Those once gorgeous silver eyes exploded in a burst of flames and incinerated his entire body. A low flying plane drowned out his screams.

He told me that Vincent owns the top floor of the Marriott Hotel in Times Square. I stood up and dusted Angel from my clothes, then took off, literally. His blood invigorated me. Soaring over my concrete jungle, the beasts below filled me with pride and strength. My intentions filled me with determination and bloodlust. And Vincent, he filled me with… RAGE!!!

I landed in a secluded alley close to 42nd street. The rain seemed to calm a little, but the thunder and lightning still tore the skies open.

Times Square was packed with reporters, movie stars, and fans. I found myself in the middle of a frenzy of flashing lights and clicking shutters. All were here for some big gala premier.

I made my way to the Marriot and snuck into a side entrance. It was a stairway that went straight up. It was hollow, sterile, and infinite, but my determination was infallible.

Angel's Blood did something to me. I could literally feel the power coursing through my body. It heightened my senses to an incredible level. I could sense what was waiting for me on that top floor. It was so clear; it was as if I were up there already.

He had maybe every vampire in the city up there outside his door. No doubt they were there waiting for me. Well I guess I shouldn't keep them waiting... It's rude you know.

I might not have demon rage anymore but righteous fury does the trick quite effectively. I switched into hyper-speed and shot straight up to the top floor. My footsteps on the stairs sounded like machine guns as they resonated through the hollow cavity; I reached the top in seconds. I halted at the door, but the velocity tore it off its hinges.

I stepped over the hunk of twisted metal and broken glass into a large open space lined end to end with red carpet filled with dozens of vampires. At the back of the room was a single door.

"Hi, my name is Sita. If you value your uh... unlives leave immediately, or I will deport you to oblivion. All of you."

They attack... I wonder why death threats never work... Oh well. I walk slowly towards them the first one charges head on then disappears behind me, I continue forward as my tail, materialized already wrapped around his neck, rips his head clean from his shoulders. It seems like they learned some things all this time I have been away because they brought weapons this time. That's fine with me... I am a weapon.

They pulled guns and knives and swords from every place that one can be concealed. They all attacked at once. One after the other they fall into pieces. I tear them limb from limb. But they persist. They are no match for me but they work to keep me from my goal. The harder they fight the more it angers me.

I can hear him on the other side of the door. There were three heartbeats coming from inside, and one of them was him. The bodies

continue to drop one after the other smacking
the ground with the wet plops of dismembered
flesh, but they keep coming. They keep me from
him; the frustration hits the boiling point. And
I scream.

"VINCENT!!!!!!"

My voice and my power causes all their
chests to cave in and their heads to explode; the
door splinters and there I stood soaked in the
blood of his minions. Rage pours from my being
and every one of their mutilated bodies bursts
into flames around me. I walk through
conflagration, tracking flaming foot prints into
the gorgeous apartment; my eyes never parting
from my prey.

The apartment was lavishly decorated and at
its center sat Vincent draining some poor girl
dry with her friend on her knees pleasuring him,
oblivious to her dead friend, she screamed when
she saw me. Vincent stood up of their own accord
my eyes dropped as he put himself away still
slick and shiny from her attentions. His lips
curl up, pleased with himself, I think. The one
girl slumped lifeless to the ground and the other
ran to a corner to find refuge, too terrified to
even scream.

"Should I wipe my feet?" I asked as I tracked blood and fire across his lily white carpet.

He stood up and walked toward me, he was wearing black silk pajama pants with no shirt or shoes. His skin was almost as white as the carpet. A small blood train ran down the side of his mouth but he licked it away before it could drip and stain his carpet. I looked into his eyes, which wasn't too much of an effort since he was only about 5'10".

He used to be beautiful, too beautiful in a way that didn't seem natural, but now I could see through it. He was handsome but normal. He tried to bespell me with his eyes but it wasn't working like before. I wasn't afraid. Ri-ight. Ok I was afraid but it was a subtle terror buried beneath anger. Anger has that fortunate tendency to make you forget how stupid you are.

"Sita, I thought you'd come looking for me," he held my chin and leaned in close, "and I'd hoped that you'd find me."

Then he ran the tip of his warm, slick tongue up my cheek licking the blood from my face. I swung around with all my speed and struck him with my tail. He flew back and out of the window, but not over the side.

I stepped out of his window onto a lush oasis artificially constructed on the roof of the Marriot. A few yards away Vincent lay on the soft grass surrounded by shattered glass. I hadn't taken my eyes off of the semi-conscious Vincent since entering the apartment but from behind me I heard my name.

"Sita..."

I spun around and there he was standing at the window looking at me. I looked back at the ground and all that lay there was broken glass.

"I can see by your look of awe that you can not begin to fathom how much..." A smirk spread across his face, as if what he was about to say tickled him, "...shit, you have gotten yourself into Little Horn. There is no way that you can possibly comprehend what I am Sita. There is no use in even talking to you anymore; it's like having to explain to a cockroach why it is unwelcome in my house. But I can show you better than I can tell you, *nena*."

The corners of his mouth turned up slightly and he said in his softest tone, "Rise..."

CHAPTER EIGHTEEN

At those words the soft dirt began to erode at my feet, and from it emerged four, four beings whose power was so immense that the air was literally dense with it. They awakened refreshed and ready to kill. All of them walked right passed me without as much as a sideways glance. The three men knelt in front of Vincent and the woman went and stood beside him.

She was all over him like a dog greeting its master, and he complemented her embrace. He turned his attention back to me while she nipped at his ear and said, "Xeno…"

The one on the right stood up. He was cloaked in a black hooded-robe, the soft, moist soil still dripping from off it. From beneath the hood two thin, jade ovals glowed like emeralds in the midnight moon.

Then Vincent said a second name, "…Sombra…"

The tall, dark-skinned beast, built like a cheetah on the left stood. He had waist length cornrows. He had a nearly visible aura pressing against my body. His eyes shimmered like obsidian.

He continued, "…Tremere…" The rain caused small sparks to flicker around him like an exposed electrical wire; his eyes, glowing white as fluorescent light bulbs, crackled; and the electricity hummed as it coursed through his body. His hair was platinum blond nearly white. Naked from the waist up, he was wearing blue jeans and no shoes. He was an undead calendar model. Electricity leaped around his body from top to bottom like a Tesla Coil.

"Call me Trey, baby," he said licking his lips, "yea I like that."

Vincent continued, "…Fauna…"

She paused from lapping small drops of blood that she has drawn from his ear lobe long enough to give me an awkward glance, the kind a newborn kitten might give to a stranger, confused yet intrigued. Her hair fell in a curly froth around her shoulders dark and beginning to shine with the rain drops. Her skin was the color of new pennies and her features strongly indigenous American. Her round irises dilated to vertical slits, and she snarled at me like an angry lioness.

"These are my lieutenants. They are second only to me in strength and power. Lords are we all. Never say I did not warn you. You will not live to see another moon. *Matala*… kill her, Xeno!"

My eyes fade to the pale blue of the devil's moonlight, while his almond shaped dragon-green eyes glimmered at the prospect of battle. The brown, modest cloak dropped to his waist, secured by a white rope, the fashion Buddhist monks wore centuries ago.

Something about him told me he knew the style personally. Beneath was a young Chinese monk. His head was shaved clean. Emblazoned across his smooth, hairless chest was the brand of The Beast, seared into his flesh, blasphemously mocking that which his form coveted. He looked about my age but his aura told of a story centuries old. He took two steps forward from across the roof then he disappeared.

He reappeared inches from my face. I had no time to react; his foot collided with the side of my head and caused me to flip and land hard on my back. I was in shock for a moment, but I regained my composure and rose slowly to my feet.

I looked him right in his emerald eyes and said, "Do it again."

He immediately obliged without so much a moments hesitation. He darted forward striking with vigor and madness. This fight was on a whole other level. He had powers that I couldn't comprehend. I couldn't get a bead on him; it wasn't speed he was actually shifting from one moment to the next, literally disappearing in between.

It was just flashes of him striking and then I would feel it. He put me on the defensive, I was forced to rely on raw speed to avoid from receiving a lethal blow, and I was just barely doing that.

Each blow he landed was insane; it was as if the force went through my body and into my souls. There was nothing for me to block or counter because there was no in between motion. I could barely breathe.

I think he'd broken some of my ribs; my chest felt like there was someone standing on it. He was so strong the air around him is heavy.

The battle seemed to draw on for hours, but at the speed we were moving I'm sure it had only been mere seconds. All I could do was bide my

time; he would make a mistake; and I was sure
of it.

He seemed unable to maintain that speed or
exertion because the length of time that he was
visible grew longer. He had finally given me
some kind of opening. I whipped my body around,
my tail split the air like a thunderbolt, but the
moment before it would have connected with his
body, he became transparent and intangible as if
he were a ghost. He disappeared laughing,
taunting me then he reappeared on all sides of me
at once. I was stunned but not ill prepared. I
just barely managed to dodge the attack.

I wasn't as clueless as he must have
thought. I noticed that he could only attack
when he is tangible and visible and that when he
is about to strike the air becomes thick like an
invisible fog. Though I couldn't see or hear him
I could still feel his presence.

I drew my trusty bone knife; I closed my
eyes so that I could see him without eyes. His
attack was ready I used my speed to get behind
him, and then I opened my eyes and began to slash
furiously in front of me. The air began to bleed
and reality slowly receded around his body.
Still screaming his head rolled off his torn,

bloody shoulders then he burst into a heap of flaming ash.

I huff as I vainly try to catch my breath. My lungs are filled with fire and my muscles are screaming. I'm going to feel this tomorrow.

I smiled at the thought.

"Heh…" Who am I kidding, I'm not going to see tomorrow

I turned to look Vincent right in the eyes, his poor attempt to mask his anger and frustration was evident. He smiled pompous.

Panting, "Heh… that all you got Vinny?"

"Impressive," he said, "I hope that exercise warmed you up because now you face Sombra, Lord of Fear and Master of Shadows."

I'm not ready.

He stood up and spoke with a deep West African accent, "Yes… young one. I am the shroud of death; I will introduce you to true pain."

I can't breath.

"Do you know why children fear the dark? You will."

My heart is racing. I'm afraid. I take in deep gasps of breath but they do nothing. This isn't from that fight. It can't be. I have been hurt worse. Had he already begun to attack?

It was the power of his voice; it had the ability to subdue. Its tone had an ominous pitch that was… frightening. I found myself entranced by mere words, and enthralled by the power in is tongue. I was so mesmerized that I didn't notice the dark hand stretching forth from his shadow.

It engulfed me in an abyss of endless darkness, black as a thousand midnights. The only light was the circle of moonlight that I stood in; outside of it was dense, black infinity. The only sounds I could hear were the endless, echoing wails that surrounded me. Moaning and crying filled my ears; I thought it was all in my head, until I heard his voice again.

"Do you hear their voices child? They are condemned spirits enjoying the pain of the darkness. Not just of my victims but yours as well. They cry for release, but they are mine because you have given them to me. And soon you will join them."

"I… don't think so," I said then I jumped from the light into the direction of his voice. But, when I got there I was met with cold, empty nothingness. The frigid air scorched my skin, and the wails tortured my souls. I could feel their sorrow, their unrest, their anger, and…

their pain. It was unbearable. I could feel
my teeth chattering and my lips beginning to ice
over: "Too… cold…"

"Yes… young one; envy, anger, passion,
they're hot. But pain and fear… cold. You have
left the safety of the light and have ventured
into the dark recesses of fear; feel it well up
inside you, until it's about to burst. Nothing
burns hotter than ice…" his voice trailed off
laughing at me.

My blood runs cold, and sweat trickles down
my face freezing in mid-air then shattering as
the droplets hit the ground. The light that I had
been standing in vanished, and then there was
only darkness. That familiar, echoing throb in
my chest that I'm so fond of began to slow; I
could feel my life slipping away. The fear began
to penetrate my senses, and chip away at my
sanity. My body felt as if it was getting
heavier and heavier; my eyelids were like lead,
it felt like… like… dying.

My eyes shut.

Then they popped open, and I was no longer
on a rooftop in New York. I wasn't even on this
side of the world. I was back in the jungle. I
was standing soaked in the rain, the thunder
bellowing high in the clouds, and the lightning

was racing across the sky. But, standing a few feet away from me in the violent torrent was a child. She couldn't have been more than ten years old.

"What are you doing out here," I asked her.

"I like the rain," she said with tears in her voice.

"Why," I asked her.

"B-Because no can tell when you're crying."

I walked over to her and knelt down next to her and asked, "But why are you crying?"

Pointing straight out in front of her she said, "Daddy…"

When I looked I saw my father looking down at me, tall, strong and confident. I was a little girl again looking up at my father as he was about to walk to his death. However, the difference this time was that I knew, and I tried to stop him.

"Daddy! Don't go in there! You're not gonna come back again!"

I had to look to the clouds to see his face. He smiled at me with his wide chin and powerful jaw. His broad nose and nostrils flared with confidence. His eyes were deep brown and filled with love. His jet black hair dripped with rainwater, and there was a lock that hung low on his forehead in wispy-carefree abandon. The sleeves of his shirt strained wrapped around his massive arms. He placed his bronze hand on my shoulder, knelt down and said in his deep, attention commanding voice.

"Sita, don't worry I always come back, and I always will. I'll be right out, I promise. Just take care of your brother for me. Ok sweetness?"

"Ok daddy, I promise."

That was the second time he broke his word. He walked inside that temple for the second time, the last time… But, it wasn't until just then that I realized that my father had just walked into the same temple that I would eventually die in.

"Oh no…"

Once I heard the door slam shut and the plank lock into place I realized that my father just walked right into the hands of the Guardian. I ran to the door and began slamming my fists against the immense stone slab. From inside I heard a familiar phrase.

"Your end is come. TIME TO DIE!!!" followed by their screams and gunshots.

"Daddiiieeeeee……" I scream.

Then there was a stillness, then blood seeped under the door.

"No, noooo..."

I dropped to my knees and closed my eyes vainly trying to stem the tide of tears. When my eyes finally decided to reopen I was greeted once again by darkness. With tears streaming down my face and freezing, I said in little more than a whisper, "That's enough."

Then I heard Sombra's voice, "No child... that is not enough. It will never be enough. The pain is so sweet and it has just begun."

I stopped hallucinating, but the voices were still there. But, of all of them, there was one that rang out as clear as crystal. The voice of a little boy, that sounded oddly familiar.

"Didn't you love me? Didn't you love me, Sita?"

I strained to see in the darkness, and a form began to take shape in the void. It was Joshua, Joshua as a child. Around his neck was a hideous scar, and he began to speak with cherub inflection.

"Why did you let him kill me Sita. I thought you promised to protect me, to love me..."

"I do love you Joshie."

"Then why are you fighting it. Just take my hand so we can be together."

Suddenly all of my men that died began to appear around him all blaming me, "It's your fault, you killed us…"

I began to back away, but I backed into something. I turned around and it was David; I wrapped my arms around him sobbing.

"I-I didn't mean to. I-It was an a-accident."

Then I heard him say, "It's… your… fault."

I slowly looked up at him and was met with a cold, lifeless face. His blood was all over my clothes, and he was eviscerated. He was completely hollowed out, then he continued, "You did this to me! Are you happy?! I told you to quit, but you *had your whole life in front of you*'," he said, mocking me, "Well where is that life now?!"

I dropped to my knees sobbing, "I'm sorry…"

I began to hyperventilate; my entire body was shaking. But there was a distant sound, past the spirits, and past the darkness. With each labored breath the sound grew louder. It was the thunder, the *real* thunder. I tried to hang onto that sound. I used it to pull me back to reality.

My breathing had begun to slow, but with each breath I could feel something building up.

The tension had reached a climax, the ultimate climax, and there was only one thing left for me to do. With one last crack of thunder I screamed.

My rage-filled screams were more fierce and terrifying than the loudest battle drum or deepest animal roar. An enormous bolt of lightning split the darkness; it used my body as a lightning rod and spread out in every direction. It sent the dark into retreat.

Smoke was rising from my body and the darkness was gone. All that remain was a single tear that ran down my face and clung, persistently, to my chin. The heat of my rage evaporated it. My eyes were luminescent, and the grass beneath me was charred.

A growl emanated from deep within me, and I charged at him quicker than night falls. I attacked him with the same malice and contempt that he had shown me. I knocked him to the ground and picked up my knife. He crawled across the ground frantically like I terrified mouse.

"I… AM… MADE… OF… RAGE!!!!" I roared.

He disappeared into his own shadow and hid among the trees in the shadows of the oasis. I tossed my knife into the shadows.

"I-It's im-impossible…" were his last
words, then a shadow on a tree materialized into
his body with the blade stuck in his forehead.
He fell off the tree and melted into a black
liquid, too thick for any bodily fluid that I
knew.

Vincent, clearly angered by the ineptitude
of his assassins was cursing softly in Spanish
under his breath. "Do not fail me."

"Come on!" I said with finality.

"Trey, Fauna *matenla ahora!*" He snarled the
words.

They begin circling me, softly growling,
"Aww did I make you mad? Hmm, were those your
friends? Honestly I thought you guys where the
strong ones. Oh well, if that's what you got
then, I'll just have to kill you and move on."

"Hey, Sita," Trey said, "Do you know what a
hundred thousand volts of electricity does to a
body."

He lifted his arms into the air and starting
at his finger tips electricity swung around his
body and slammed into the ground. The long,
crooked fingers grasped for my legs, but I leapt
to safety. That "safety" however, landed me in
the clutches of an angry lioness. I looked up
and there she was standing over me, ready to snap

my head off. She snarled trying to avulse me
of flesh, but I dodged just in time to avoid her
powerful jaws.

"Where the hell did that come from," I
shouted as I got to my feet.

"Hey…" I heard from behind me. I turned and
Trey was right behind me. He grabbed my throat
and started to electrocute me.

"You know first the synapses in your brain
begin to fire all at once. You can't think
straight. Then all of your muscles tighten. You
lose control of all bodily function," he charges
his free hand, "but you won't start to die yet.
Your heart will compensate as long as…" he puts
that charged hand right on top of my heart, "no
electricity passes through your chest."

I could feel my brain short-circuiting; all
my thoughts were scrambled. My heart wanted to
explode.

I'm dying.

There was only one impulse that I could
decipher from the jumbled thoughts, "*I have to
get him off of me…*"

"Let… me… GO!"

It was instinct that sent my knee right
between his legs then training that told me to
follow up with an uppercut to his nose. As I

tried to regain my senses I could hear from
behind me the sounds of bones scraping, and the
wet popping as they reconfigured themselves. I
spun around and the lioness had transformed. Now
what stood before me was an immense goliath. It
was a bear bigger than any I have ever seen. It
wasn't any specific type it kind of was just all
of them in one.

I suddenly felt a jolt repelling me away
from Trey as if we were magnets of the same poles
and towards the bear. I saw the smile on his
face and the glow in his eyes told me that the
force was coming from him. I turned and was shot
in to the arms of the massive beast, and by the
way if you have never been bear hugged by an
actual bear, I wouldn't recommend it; it's not as
pleasant as they would have you believe.

Even with my supernatural physique I was
grid locked within the colossus' gigantic body.
My lungs would have burst if instinct had not
taken over.

My wings involuntarily manifested themselves
and expanded; Fauna lost her grip and released
me. Then my wings returned to their resting
place within my body, their task having been
accomplished. I knelt on the ground on my hands
and knees taking in deep gasps of breath, but

before I could recover I heard her bellow then she swiped me with her ham-sized paw.

After that I don't think that I had any more ribs intact as I slid across the roof and into the small lagoon in the middle of the oasis. The pain made my body feel like it was made of stone, and being curled up clutching my ribs I sunk to the bottom like a brick. I began to feel the ground quake as the hellish creature galloped across the roof. She leapt high into the air and reverted back to her original form, but the water invoked in her another transformation. Before my eyes she became the Queen of the Deep; a predator so perfect that in that in a thousand millennia it has remained unchanged, The Great White. I grabbed for my knife but it wasn't on my belt.

I nearly panicked...

"AAAAHHHHH..."

GARGLE

Ok so I did panic.

I swam frantically for the surface; I needed air. She lunged forward trying to grab my ankle, but I avoided her attempt and dove to the bottom. I looked up and saw her diving straight down at me, but past her, out of the water I saw Trey leap onto a branch overlaying the surface.

He paused obviously waiting for me to surface for air. I spent too much time looking at him because I suddenly felt a myriad of serrated blades sink into my thigh. I winced then tried to scream but it came out as a deep throated moan.

She whipped me around in the water trying to tear my leg off. The water took on a crimson hue; through the scarlet fog my fists connect with her nose, but her grip was unwavering. I searched with my fingers and found an eye. I jabbed my finger into it and felt the rubbery orb burst.

She finally released her crushing vice-grip and began hysterically thrashing around in the water. I made my way to the surface, but just as I was about to gasp for some desperately need oxygen I felt her hand clasp around my ankle. She yanked me back below the surface, but just then my soles hardened; my toes fused and I mule-kicked her in the head with my hooves.

The surface tension grew taut then exploded as I forced myself through its cohesive skin. I landed on the branch behind Trey; he turned his hands glowing, charging up for some electrical attack.

"AAH, don't touch me," I scream as I ejected him from the tree with a hoof to the stomach.

"He fell toward the water screaming, "No… Nooooo!!!"

"Oooo… sorry about that, you scared me," I yelled.

As soon as he splashed into the water, as everyone knows from grade school chemistry, electricity reacts violently when introduced to water. There was a short pause… before all the cells of his body de-ionized then evacuated all of their electrical contents simultaneously. Upon evacuation every atom of his body exploded at the speed of light, and he erupted beneath the surface with volcanic force. But instead of fire and magma spewing from the lagoon there was just pure electricity.

The shockwave knocked me from the branch and the explosion incinerated the second abomination beneath the water. All the electrical bolts fused into one tremendous lightning bolt and shot straight up into the clouds.

The thunder roared and the calming shower kicked up again. It was once again a torrential downpour, alone on the roof now just him and me, our eyes never parting from each others.

My hand barely shakes.

CHAPTER NINTEEN

"The games are over! Now you die!!" I
shouted. I switched into hyper-speed and charged
him teeth bared, claws clenched and over
confident…

He began to move, attempting to avoid my
attack, but he was already too slow. It brought
a small smirk to my face, but that soon
disappeared when I realized that he was making a
fool of me. The moment before I connected with
him his speed increased to the infinite degree.
I found myself charging a dark silhouette of his
body.

There was a small flash and a whoosh as the
air and light rushed in to fill the empty space
that he left. He had side stepped and grabbed me
by the throat in mid-air. He lifted me over his
head and his voice assumed a Demonic tone.

"You were always so thick headed Morrigan! You still don't listen to reason! I cannot be killed! I cannot be harmed! And no one short of God himself can possibly comprehend what I have become, especially not a petty, demon-whore. You asked me once if this was Hell. Abandon hope all ye who enter, for you *are* in Hell, and I am the Devil."

He punched me in my chest, effectively caving it in. I spat blood on his hand and he laughed. He walked over to the edge of the roof then punched me in the face breaking my nose. I saw black and white starbursts.

He waited for it to heal and then he broke it again. My stomach wrenched and I knew he gave me a concussion.

He pulled my face close to his and said, "Just like old times."

Then he kissed me and licked the blood from my lips. I would have gagged but his grip on my throat was too tight, so I spat bloody mucus into his face.

The last thing he said was a message, "And I wept as a *child* would... for naught, save the Beast, was there for me to see..."

He set me down on my feet right on the ledge of the roof. "You will die… screaming," I said knowing what was coming next, "I promise."

Then he pushed me and as I flew from the ledge I could hear his maniacal laughter echo all the way down. On the ground there was a pool, but that provided no measure of relief because from the height at which I fell I would hit the bottom regardless.

My eyes, which had been open the entire way down, burst on contact with the water then I slammed into the floor of the pool. My organs liquefied and every bone in my body was shattered. The impact knocked me unconscious, and I fell into a void of endless anguish. Every inch of my body was on fire, every cell scorched, and every nerve blistered; but the one piece of reality that kept me from dying was Vincent's message. I knew where he was going and what he was planning to do when he got there. That fact snapped me back into consciousness.

I was underwater and my collapsed lungs were being filled with the chlorine saturated liquid. The pain was intense, too intense. I threw up under water and a cloud of blood, vomit, and teeth surrounded my head. The sound of rain and short bursts of thunder echoed under the water,

and resonated in the hollow cavity that was
once my face. Through the pain there began a
surprising, but familiar sound, my heartbeat. I
felt coursing through my body mostly my blood,
but also something not nearly as familiar,
Angel's blood! It began to saturate every ounce
of my broken body; my bones began to mend on
their own. My contorted spine straightened, the
mangled bones in my face began to knit, and my
shattered ribcage started to reconstruct. Though
the pain was helpful it was still immense, and I
blacked out again. However, this time I knew
that I would reawaken. The Abyss returned.

I could hear the rain and thunder, but they
were now accompanied by my own muffled screams.
Seconds in reality were an eternity of pain, but
my screaming started to become more and more
distant while the rain grew louder. It got
louder and louder until… a burst of heaven
trembling lightning tore the sky open. The
thunder shot through me and my eyes popped open.

I was under water but I was not dead.

Surrounded by blood, bones, and shattered
linoleum I was snatched from the water by a cop.
He began to administer CPR when I shouted, "Get
off of me! I'm okay!"

"I'm sorry ma'am. I saw you fall from the roof into the pool. I thought for sure that you were dead but then I saw you moving. I can't believe you survived that…"

I interrupted him pleasantly surprised, "Officer Andrade?! Hiya' Nick."

"O-OH M-MY G-G-GOD!!!" He stammered, "No… get away. You're not real. Don't kill me!!!" He turned and ran.

That wasn't very polite, I mean I did let him live, oh well.

A crowd had gathered. Each face was amazed at what they were witnessing. The spectacle of celebrities and such paled in comparison to my swan dive from the Marriot Hotel. Just to add to it I spread my wings and shot up into the air.

There was a collective gasp and I heard someone exclaim, "This movie gon' be hawt!"

I landed on the roof and walked into Vincent's house. When I entered both girls were dead and cold. The face of the one that was still alive when I arrived was twisted with terror, frozen in that expression of her last horrible moments.

I don't even want to imagine what he must have done to her. I stepped back out onto the oasis as the sun was rising. It dispersed me and

David was standing right in front of me. That
vision of him in the darkness popped back into my
head and I recoiled.

"Whoa!" he said, "it's okay. It's me, it's
me."

"Oh God… you were… Oh God…"

He saw the tears welling up in my eyes and
he grabbed me and pulled me close, then he said,
"Its okay, I know. I saw what happened."

"It's my fault," I said.

"What?"

"Everything! All of this is happening
because of me. David I killed us," I shouted
with a knot in my throat.

"No, no. I saw what he did to you. None of
that was real. It was an illusion. None of it
was your fault; everything happened as it was
meant to. Without our sacrifices Nicco could not
have been born. I told you this would not be
easy."

"I-I tried… I-I…"

"Forget it. There is nothing that did not
happen as it was supposed to, but you have to
finish it. Vincent cannot reach Nicco before
he's ready or the war is over before it has had a
chance to begin."

"So I have to kill Vincent."

"Yes and as you noticed the old ones have powers beyond understanding. They can put you through all levels of hell. The older they become, the more they evolve and Vincent is the oldest. As insane as the powers of those lieutenants were Vincent is the oldest and strongest; he trumps them all. Be prepared to encounter the true Usher of Hell."

"Damn..."

No sooner was I back before I heard someone yell, "POLICE, DON'T MOVE!"

I had to reappear in the middle of a crime scene, *sigh*.

I was in front of a virtual firing squad and there was no explaining what I was doing here, so...

I ran.

I ran through the haze of bullets as they opened fire and leapt over the edge of the roof this time I managed to get my wings open. I flew straight up and the force knocked them all down.

"Whoa!!!" One them exclaimed.

"I can't believe that just f*cking happened!!!"

I knew where Vincent was going and I was hoping that I had arrived before him; it was a

short distance as the Succubus flies. I landed
in Vanessa's backyard and the back door was open.

"God don't let me be too late," I whispered.

I went in and called out desperately,
"Vanessa! Vanessa! Where are you!?! Please,
answer!"

Then from the living room I heard the
television:

"*A double homicide rocks Times Square. Two
young girls slain...*"

I shut the television off; both Vanessa and
Nicco were soundly asleep on the couch, much to
my relief. I went back out to the back yard.
The sky was so clear, so beautiful, every star
was out. I walked over to the lonely tree in the
center of the yard. Using my knife I carved the
last words to my child in its base:

"*There is a place between asleep and awake;
it's the place where you still remember dreaming.
That is where I'll always love you and that is
where I'll always be.*

–Mom"

"My will is shred and forsaken; I am undone
by eternal blasphemy..."

I spun around knowing instinctually what I
was about to encounter. Vincent with his hand

clutched over Vanessa's throat, who was crying as she held Nicco.

My hand doesn't shake at all.

She tried to speak, "I'm sorry, Sita. I-I…"

He squeezed tighter until all that came out was a hoarse squeak.

"Sita," he said with a jovial tone, "It is surprising to see you. It wasn't nearly so hard to kill Morrigan. You are very persistent, ah well. Your power is very impressive. No one as ever survived an encounter with my acolytes, let alone killed any of them. But you, you murdered them with a measure of grace. But don't make the mistake of believing that because you were able to kill them that you have a chance against me. You know nothing of my power. But do not worry I am tired of trying to kill you; I realized just how much I missed you. I loved you once. Once I execute the Avatar you and I can once again rule side by side."

After he finished his little rant he began to blow a kiss, and he had already pushed me over the edge.

"Arrogant Bastard!!!" I screamed as I lunged at him trying to tear his tongue out.

But that kiss he blew was no ordinary kiss. It was filled with darkness. It was like

slamming into a brick wall. His breath made
some sort of barrier that repelled me all the way
across the yard. He threw Vanessa to the ground
and then the ground began to shake.

He began chuckling as his voiced changed
into its true form. He embodied Hell. It flowed
through him so freely that you could see it and
hear it and feel it. The grass blackened at his
feet and a swell of evil poured off of him, "I am
the morning and the evening star. Darkness is my
mistress and all her children bow down before me.
Those who don't will be condemned and you Sita
will know me. I am your Lord and I will lay my
wrath upon thee."

"Um… No."

I think I might have pissed him off; his
rage exploded into a red flame as his fury
erupted and he lunged at me. I managed to barely
dodge before he connected, but he landed with the
agility of a jaguar. The ground where he landed
concaved under the stress of his power.

He began to laugh and I asked, "What is so
funny? I like to laugh too."

"You were not so quick when I found you in
that alley nearly a year ago. The progress
you've made is astounding. What has come over
you?"

Besides my resolve the other influence that I keep feeling is Angel. I don't know why but his blood saved me more than once, and since I drained that boy I have felt more powerful.

"Angel?! I knew that you killed him, but how could that insect's blood make you this powerful?"

"What?!" I exclaimed, "I didn't say anything about Angel."

He began laughing again as he circled me licking his lips, "Come now, *nena,* your thoughts come to me as clearly as if they came from your own lips."

"He has to be joking," I thought.

"Does it look like I'm joking, *bella,*" he replied.

"Get out of my head!" I rebuked.

He laughed again then he attacked. Fighting him was like trying to fight the Devil himself. The earth shifted and the ground eroded. His power was so dark and evil. The sky above the house was as dark as pitch; the stars hid in fear; and the moon couldn't bear to show her face. I was completely abandoned.

A dark wave shot from his body and ran through me like black rain, and my entire body became like lead. He made his fingernails extend

all at once and they glimmered with a metallic
luster. His speed forced time itself to slow as
if it needed catch its breath.

I felt a sharp sting across my chest and
face, and it burned. It burned me to my soul,
both of them. We both screamed at the same time
and I dropped to my knees. Then I felt four
thin blades scorch my back; my skin blistered and
split.

I screamed towards high heaven and I seemed
to regain the stars' attention. They reappeared
and the universe suddenly felt an obligation, The
Force seemed to suddenly care. The cosmos which
had been an ocean of eternity was reduced to
nothing more now than a shallow glass of water.
A glass from which I was coerced to drink; and
drink I did. Two souls became one energy, and
one body became essence. My eyes faded, my mouth
watered, and my wings unfolded.

I was ready to kill.

CHAPTER TWENTY

He charged me and I folded my wings in front
of me creating a shield which stopped him in his
tracks. Then I clapped them together, the
resulting shockwave propelled him to the other
end of the yard and blood streamed down from his
eyes and ears.

He looked at me with bloody tears then
disappeared behind me, but I spun around and
sliced him in half with my tail. I spun a full
360 degrees and ended up with my back to him.
After disemboweling him my body reverted back to
normal.

I awaited the customary scream and burst,
but it never came. Instead I heard Vincent's
unmistakable laughter. I slowly turned around
and I felt my heart throbbing in my chest. He
wasn't anywhere to be seen and his cackle echoed
in the night; then I felt a tap on my shoulder.

I turned and was welcomed with a kick to
my mid-section. A long, strained groan was heard
as all the air rushed out of my body. I dropped
to my hands and knees gasping for air. Then he
kicked me again in the ribs, and I skidded across
the ground until I slammed into the base of the
tree that I had carved into and the one that
Vanessa and Nicco now used as sanctuary from
Vincent's onslaught. Nicco started crying and
the ground began to tremble again. Vincent
walked over to me.

Wind started to blow and it took me a second
to realize that the wind was coming from him as
was the smell that it carried. The odor was not
something that I recognized but with her
centuries of death and carnage for experience
Morrigan did.

It was the smell of corpses, rotting in the
sun, bloated bodies cracking open spilling black
putrid fluids on the ground. I gagged and threw
up.

His eyes glowing blood red, his clothes torn
to shreds and charred, his muscles strained, his
skin now beyond pale almost transparent and
glowing, I could see the blue veins snaking their
way through him and his jet-black hair held aloft
by his own power.

A hellish red aura surrounded his body; he smiled flashing his long dagger-like fangs, a smile that went all the way to his eyes, true happiness. His eyes were completely black, shining with no white showing like giant pupils. Rats have eyes like that. I'm not ashamed to say, his smile was less than soothing. This was his true power. It was of Hell, and it was terrifying.

Then he said, "You-can't-beat-me," each word punctuated by a stomp to my head, the snaps of my bones were drowned out by the deafening impact of his blows. He drew his fist high preparing to end it.

"In his wake I lay strewn, my soul rent asunder, condemned I still weep for he…"

I blocked his death blow, and doused his fiery eyes with my cool azure gaze as I stood up refusing to accept this fate a second time. No not this time.

"For he will *never* defeat me."

I think I pissed him off again because he punched me again and my body slammed into the tree and it cracked. Then he hit me again and it cracked some more then again and it cracked a little more, but I rejected the urge to fall back down.

Through all the pain I began to laugh. He stopped his assault and frowned at me, "What could you possibly find so amusing? You are going to Hell."

I didn't even dignify him with a response; I just continued to laugh, harder. He grabbed me by the throat.

"Why are you laughing!?! Do you think this is a joke? Or are you mocking me?"

I looked up at him broken and bleeding then said, "Sniff up Vincent. Do you smell that intoxicating aroma? It smells like a fresh rainfall, roses, and vanilla all rolled into one; that Vincent, is the sunrise."

His eyes widened and reverted to normal. His power subsided and he looked down at me with defeat in his eyes before he could even comprehend the concept.

"N-no. It can't be. I am invincible. I am God!"

A small pained smile came to my face because for once he actually realized what he was in the true scheme of things, a weak, insignificant, finite… mortal. But that, to him, was unacceptable; he extended his fingernails and the fire in his eyes glowed hotter and brighter than it ever had. The light reflected off his nails and cast a shadow on his face revealing his inner demon. He no longer even resembled a human.

"If I go to Hell you're coming with me! I'll look forward to tormenting you for eternity."

"It doesn't work that way," I boasted, "while you'll be rotting in Hell, I'll be watching from Heaven. But don't fret I'll make sure that they have a nice hot spike for you to sit on when you get there."

That was the last of his sanity, he snapped, "Not if I can help it, *BITCH!*"

He lunged at me with all the speed he could muster, trying to slash my throat. But the sun was that much faster. His hand went right through me, because all he connected with was dense, foggy mist. The sun ignited his hand first then flame crept slowly up his arm; allowing him to feel every inch burn. Feral animal shrieks and demonic bellows of agonizing pain welled up in him then erupted; the glass windows of the house shattered and car alarms went off as he wailed. He dropped to his knees and the fire engulfed him.

"No, No, AHHH!!!!!"

Every soul listening could hear his shrieks. Even as a charred corpse his screams would not cease. It wasn't until his bones crumbled to dust and his smoldering ashes blew away that there was finally peace. All that remained of him was his blackened skull, which at last disintegrated. But, from its ashes grew a divine rose bush, whose roses bore no thorns, and whose petals never fell.

It was immortal.

EPILOGUE

The sky was gray with the morning fog just before the onset of dawn. It created a beautiful backdrop over the city, and on an anonymous rooftop in the middle of the largest city in the world there was a speck. The speck danced in the morning wind; to and fro; yonder and hither. One who would try to make sense from its movements or try to find purpose in its ramblings would go mad. It appeared to be going nowhere, but everywhere at once. It would go up but yet again it would go down. To a watching bystander it was nothing that required more than half a thought, but to the alert Observer it created an intricate design, a design with striking familiarity. The speck soon became a spark, and trailing with it a flame. It was a minute comet, a blip on a planet that has a billion and one things going on at any given moment. The tail trailing the spark began to take form. At first it was not more than an amorphous flame floating in mid-air. The Observer became fully aware of what the flame was imitating. The physics of it were impossible, the mathematics beyond complex, and the probability of it infinitesimal. It was imitating the creation of life. Dawn's first sun-kiss shot across the horizon and cast a silhouette on the figure standing on the rooftop. He turned to face the rising sun; it reflected in eyes deprived of it for centuries and he whispered to himself, "I'm back."